The Man from Grapalia

The Mason Braithwaite Paranormal
Mystery Series, book 8

In this series:

Signs Point to Yes

The Desert Rats

Reach for the Sky

Billy Blood

Rubber-Band Ball

The Invisible Arrow

Penstock Canyon

The Man from Grapalia

The Mythical Blond

Stealth Glasses

The Melted Pineapple

Night on the Water

The Landers Mystique

Praise for the series:

Every foray by Church's wonderful psychic
detective Mason Braithwaite is a truly
suspenseful page-turner in the most unusual
crime series ever, and certainly one that no
aficionado of crime fiction should miss.
—David Osborn, author of the best-selling
thrillers *The French Decision*
and *Love and Treason*

Another fast-paced ride through Los Angeles
by Church, who continues to reinvent and
reinvigorate Mason Braithwaite. Church's
writing is vivid, the worlds he creates believable,
and his characters have a breadth of humanity,
strength, and vulnerability that makes the series
a fun-filled, page-turning adventure.
—Jeremy Randolph, author of *The Mural*

Mason is a hero like none who have come
before him: a sensitive, queer P.I. whose only
weapon is his intuition. This book turns the
detective genre on its head and makes you
think about the ninety percent of your brain
you're not using.
—Teja Watson, author of *Attic.doc*

Thanks to Christopher Church for giving us
another exciting and well written adventure
with one of my new heroes.
—Amos Lassen

The Man from Grapalia

The Man from Grapalia

Christopher Church

DAGMAR
MIURA
LOS ANGELES

Published by Dagmar Miura
Los Angeles
www.dagmarmiura.com

The Man from Grapalia

First published 2018

ISBN: 978-1-942267-62-1

One

On a gritty stretch of Olympic Boulevard, at the fringes of Koreatown, Mason steeled himself to meet Anna, whose storefront assailed the neighborhood in huge white letters: PSYCHIC. In the window below, PALM READING glowed in neon block letters, glaring harshly in the afternoon light. Mason had worked with her before, as they both used their psychic skills to earn a living, albeit in divergent ways. This time he'd been summoned here, ostensibly because she had a client to refer to him.

Pulling open her front door, he ducked to avoid hitting the little bell hung above, safely over the heads of most people, but Mason was tall, and had a different perspective on things. He waited in the cramped front room, lit by the glare of the neon— she'd certainly heard the bell, and she'd call him when she was ready. There were a pair of armchairs, facing each other for quick readings, and an incongruous poster on the wall: a fuzzy flying saucer with the caption KEEP YOUR EYES ON THE SKIES. Immediately through the heavy purple curtains into the back doorway was her consult room, Mason knew, where she read palms, tarot cards, and even a crystal ball, when clients wanted it.

It didn't take long. A meaty arm parted the purple fabric, followed by Anna's smiling face. She was dressed for work—a low-cut red caftan, a scarf covering her hair, a chunky crystal necklace that sparkled in the light.

"My favorite redhead," she said, her Eastern European accent flattening the vowels. "In Russia they say 'There was never a saint with red hair.'"

"What's that supposed to mean?" he demanded, putting his hands on his hips. He hated that his hair was the first thing people noticed about him.

"It means that redheads are temperamental."

"Maybe because we get called out so often," he said, forcing a smile. He didn't want to start off irritated with her—especially if there might be money to be made.

Anna waved an arm to dismiss the matter. "My niece is expecting a client. We can talk at the teahouse." She pushed out the front door of the shop onto the sidewalk, blinking at the daylight.

Mason walked with her down the block to a little Korean restaurant. They sat near the window, Mason sliding off his backpack and hanging it on the back of his chair. Anna ordered something in Korean.

"Can I get some kimchi, but without any fish?" Mason asked the waitress. "And whatever pickled veggies you've got." When she'd gone, he said to Anna, "This is a treat. I never get down here."

She nodded. "One of the perks of the neighborhood."

The waitress set down barley tea for both of them, and Anna took a delicate sip.

Mason wrapped his hands around the warm cup. "So why am I here, Anna?"

She set down her tea and leaned toward him. "I work for a woman named Margaret Whitby. Very wealthy. She's a regular client—I do tarot readings for her at her house. She likes to talk to her dead husband. It's nothing dramatic," she said, waving her arm. "I give her vague readings, and she gets reassurance that he's OK."

"Do you really talk to him?" Mason asked.

She paused as the waitress set down a plate of elegantly cut rice and seaweed rolls for Anna and Mason's array of pickles.

"I provide general information from beyond the veil," she said, looking down at her plate. "And encouragement to engage with the world. You know how it is."

"Why do you need me?" he asked, plucking at

the kimchi with his chopsticks. "I don't do readings."

"Something has come up that's out of my depth. It sounded more like your kind of work. One of Margaret's cousins has arrived from Europe. I think he's from a parallel world."

Mason frowned. "What does that mean?"

She munched her roll, holding his gaze. "His passport is from a country that doesn't exist. There's no trace of it online."

"How did he get into the country with that?"

"I don't know the details," she said, returning to her food. "Margaret is anxious to understand it, and I don't have the means to help her."

"You said he's a cousin. She's met him before?"

"That's the thing—he's a distant relative from overseas, and they've been corresponding recently, but they'd never met."

"Is she suspicious that it's some kind of trick?"

"Of course. That was her first instinct. But the purpose of a con job is usually to get someone's money, and he showed up with his own."

"So what would the job entail?" Mason asked. "Either she believes him, or she doesn't."

"She wants to know whether it's true or not. Is there a parallel world that people can travel from?"

"I have no idea."

"But you could do the research. Margaret doesn't know whether to believe it or not. This man is flustered at the situation, upset that his home-land is gone. But he knows a lot about her family, so his tale seems at least plausible."

"Parallel worlds," Mason said, sipping his tea. "It's definitely intriguing. I could look into it."

"Good. I have an appointment with her tomorrow morning. You can go in my place." She fished in her bra for her phone, which made Mason glance away, his cheeks reddening—though it didn't seem to embarrass Anna at all. She tapped and swiped at the device and then recited an address.

Mason reached around for his backpack and pulled out a yellow notepad and a pen. "I've never heard of that street. Where is it?"

"Hollywood Hills. Way up, near Mulholland."

"How do you spell her name?" he asked, scribbling down the details.

Anna gestured for the bill as he was writing. When the waitress set it on the table, she reached inside her caftan again, groping around her ample bosom.

"Let me buy," Mason said quickly, glancing up. "I appreciate the referral."

She nodded assent and rose, wandering out to the street while Mason pulled his wad of cash out of his pants and dropped some bills on the table.

"Give yourself plenty of time to drive up there," she said as they walked back to her shop. "It's on one of those crazy winding one-lane streets."

"Not a problem on two wheels," he said, nodding to his bicycle.

She glanced at it dubiously. "You might want to take a taxi. It's far."

He waved good-bye, watching her go back

inside before unlocking his ride. That neon sign was so obnoxious. So bright, so intrusive, when their work itself was just the opposite—all about what was hidden, subtleties and nuances teased out of nothingness, the airy strands of extrasensory inspiration.

The last few blocks of the ride home were always the hardest, pedaling uphill from the boulevard, and he still got winded despite doing it daily for years. Wheeling his bike into the garage, he saw that both of Ned's cars were here, which meant he was home.

Ned was a great guy to come home to. He provided Mason with a lot of stability, even though he was skeptical about the real nature of Mason's psychic work. But they'd learned to navigate around that, mostly because Mason had decided he didn't need his boyfriend to be a complete believer.

Walking in the front door, Mason was disappointed not to be greeted by the smell of cooking when it was this close to dinnertime. Low in the west, the sun streamed through the balcony railing and in the French doors, the hazy marine layer finally having burned off. Ned was in the kitchen, apron on, brandishing a zucchini.

"How was your meeting?" he asked.

"Great—I got a lead on a job." Mason leaned across the countertop to kiss him hello. Ned was half a head shorter and infinitely more polished than Mason, his clothes looking freshly pressed even now, at the end of the day. Coils of green were piled on the countertop. Shaved zucchini, he realized. "What are you making?"

"Pesto and zucchini noodles. How does that sound?"

"Amazing," he said, thankful that Ned's passion for vegan cooking never seemed to wane. "Do you need help?"

"I don't think so. It'll be an hour or so."

It was just as well; Mason's ineptitude around kitchen tools, especially the sharp ones, meant he got to skate on food prep. He went down the hall to the office he shared with Ned and sat at his desk. Peggy's bedroom door was closed, but he could hear the soft strumming of her guitar. Their roommate worked for lawyers to make a living, but music was her passion, and when she was practicing or composing her mellow folk music, it made for a relaxed mood in the house.

He took his notepad out of his backpack and tore off the page of notes he'd made with Anna, reading through them and then slipping them into a manila folder. Pulling open his laptop, he searched for the name Whitby, and soon found a likely match, an old Los Angeles family that came up in news stories about philanthropy. There was a nonprofit bearing the Whitby name, of course; the very wealthy routinely used charitable foundations as a tax dodge. Some of them did truly philanthropic work, he knew, but others were mainly about amassing wealth and maintaining the assets.

The foundation's website revealed the name of the family's patriarch, Cyrus Whitby, described as a "distiller and vintner." A more objective site that covered LA's motley history described the Whitbys in detail. More than just a booze maker, Cyrus had parked a boat in the Pacific during prohibition—technically in international waters and so just beyond the reach of U.S. law, but only a few miles off the California coast—shuttling partiers and gamblers out to spend money. It was a lucrative setup, charging premium rates for otherwise unobtainable and illegal goods and services and paying no taxes. After alcohol was legalized again in 1933, Cyrus went into the legitimate booze business.

Sketching on his notepad, Mason diagrammed the family tree, and soon figured out that Anna's Margaret Whitby must be the widow of Cyrus's grandson, the one who'd diversified the family business and set up the philanthropic foundation. Newspaper stories implied that Margaret's son ran the business today, even though in several instances she was still referred to as the "matriarch." Mason estimated that Margaret was in her early seventies, although he wasn't able to find a photo of her.

He looked up, startled, when Peggy came into the office.

"Hungry?" she asked, smiling at his surprise. She was wearing sweatpants and a rumpled T-shirt, her long brown hair tied behind her head.

"On my way," he said, tearing off his notes

about the Whitbys and sliding them into a manila folder.

Peggy propped the French doors open for the cool evening air, and the three of them sat at the dining table. The vegan pesto was perfect, as always.

"This is so good," Mason said, twirling zucchini noodles around his fork. "Have either of you ever heard of an old LA family called Whitby?"

Ned shook his head, and Peggy said, "No—why?"

"I might do some work for one of them. The matriarch. They got rich as rumrunners during prohibition, then later made booze legally. There's a charitable foundation with their name on it."

"That means they have serious money," Peggy said. "What are you going to do for them?"

"Some long-lost relative showed up."

"From where?" Peggy said.

"A country that doesn't exist, so it must be in a parallel world."

"Here we go," Ned said, his brow furrowed. "What evidence is there for that?"

Mason could see he was struggling not to pass instant judgment, even though that was his instinct. Ned was a hard-core nontheist, with little tolerance for anything outside the realm of the tangible.

Mason explained what little he knew, about the confused visitor with the strange passport.

"How old is matriarch Margaret?" Ned asked.

"In her seventies."

"Then it's a scam," Ned said. "This mystery guy is trying to fleece a rich old woman."

"Maybe," Mason agreed. "But Anna said he has his own money. Also, parallel worlds aren't that far-out."

Ned snorted, pesto-drenched noodles dangling from his fork.

Mason shot him a look. "It's part of mainstream physics now. I just read something about our gravity leaking into other dimensions."

"I'm not skeptical that there are other worlds—I'm skeptical that someone could step between them and into a rich woman's lap."

Mason nodded. Ned had a point.

"So you're both coming on Thursday, I hope?" Peggy said, her tone brightening.

"I bought tickets as soon as you told us about it," Ned said.

"You said it's not music, but are you still doing Peggy Pregnant?" Mason asked.

Her stage persona was an extremely pregnant folk singer, dressed in flower-child garb, who performed while cradling her guitar in front of the massive strap-on baby bump. For years she'd played small clubs and coffeehouses around town, and no one ever asked why she hadn't had the baby yet.

"Not this time," she said. "It's new territory for me—pure performance."

"What does that involve?"

Peggy grinned. "You'll have to come and find out."

After he'd helped clean up, Mason did some more reading, sprawled comfortably on the sofa with Ned, who was engrossed in his tablet. Peggy left to spend the night at her boyfriend's place, which meant Mason and Ned could have sex without worrying about making noise.

Later, as Mason was drifting into the hypnagogic state, he found himself running along a rooftop, balancing on the peak, the shingled surface dropping away dramatically on both sides. Something was chasing him, but he didn't know what, and he couldn't afford to stop or even look back for fear of getting thrown off balance. Now he was approaching the void, the precarious end of the structure. Just beyond was another rooftop, terrifyingly far away, but he knew he had to jump, that he couldn't hesitate or falter, or all would be lost. He threw himself into the air, arms and legs flailing, hoping he would make it across.

Waking with a start, his heart pounding, he looked around the dark room to make sure that, yes, it had been a dream. But was there something else? It had pulled him out of sleep—a noise, or a voice. He listened for a minute, head still swimming in grogginess, but there was only Ned's rhythmic breathing and the muted rumble of the city beyond the window.

Climbing out of bed, careful not to wake his partner, he stepped over to the floor mirror. He could just make out his own naked body, hazy in the scant illumination from the window. Not long ago, up in Penstock Canyon, the little people, the *chaneques,* had shown him how to talk to his reflection and get it to answer. It was a technique to access some part of his subconscious—manifested as the illusion of interacting with his own reflection—as he'd had to sink into an altered state of mind to do it. He was near that state now, he realized, drifting in shifted awareness, staring at himself.

"I can see your junk," his reflection said, and giggled.

The skin on the back of his neck prickled, but he didn't recoil. This wasn't entirely unexpected. "Did you call me?" he asked. "I woke up, and here you are."

"For some reason I'm really empowered right now," his reflection said, shifting his weight from one foot to the other. It was disconcerting, as if his reflection had become something else, a recording that he was watching. "You should let me out of here."

"What?" Mason said, his voice rising. "Why would I do that?"

"I could help you."

"To do what?" he demanded, trying to keep his voice down. He glanced over at the bed to make sure he hadn't woken Ned.

"I don't know, but I think it's why I'm here. I'm so energized." His reflection glanced around the room and did a neck roll. Mason could hear his joints crack. "It's actually pretty easy. You do a séance—you need three people. And a mirror, of course."

"And then you'd be running around, like a

copy of me?" Mason asked. "That doesn't make any sense."

"It wouldn't be for long. There's not enough energy for me to become a full-on permanent person."

"What?"

"I'd have an expiration date."

The whole idea was disturbing, and there was no reason even to consider such a thing. But he asked, "How long would you be here?"

"I'm not sure. A few days."

"What happens to you then? You crawl back into the mirror?"

"I assume I wouldn't exist anymore. I might hang on as a remnant in your psyche or something."

"Isn't that terrifying?"

His reflection shrugged. "Not to me. It is for you people because you're so attached to waking consciousness. I'm fine with sinking back into the essence."

Mason sighed. "I don't think I'd want to bring you here."

"I'm just *you*," he said emphatically. "What could go wrong?"

"It's too weird."

His reflection scoffed. "'Weird' is basically your job description." They watched each other for a few seconds, and then his reflection gestured toward the bed. "Why don't you sleep on it?" With a louche grin, he added, "Although if that guy was in my bed, I wouldn't be doing much sleeping."

Mason stepped toward the bed, forcing his eyes away from the mirror, and climbed back in. He lay there for a while, trying to think clearly about what had just happened. But sleep soon took over, and hardly noticing, he sank deep into unconsciousness.

Two

It always put Mason in a dark mood to wake to an alarm, but that was the messed-up reality of how the world worked. He dragged himself out of bed and pulled on a pair of boxer shorts and a T-shirt, stumbling out to the kitchen to get the espresso machine working. The house was quiet, Ned already gone, probably to have lunch with his parents after Sunday mass. Why was he so tired? The memory of talking to his reflection flooded into his awareness. It felt dreamlike now, but he knew it had been real, and in the clear light of day it still made him feel uneasy.

Pushing it out of his mind, he poured the whole pot of espresso into a mug and sat at the counter, munching on some apricots. They were soft and juicy, the stone easy to pluck out. After a bowl of muesli, starting on his second pot of coffee, he carried his mug into the office and spent a few minutes figuring out how to get to Margaret Whitby's place. Looking at a map online, he couldn't decide whether to approach it from Hollywood or keep going on the metro under the hill and cycle back from the Valley side. Anna was right—it was way up there, and either way it was going to be a difficult uphill ride. The Valley, he decided finally. Even though it was a little farther, the inclines weren't as steep.

Zooming in to look at the street, he saw only a solid metal gate with treetops beyond, but the aerial photos showed a several sizeable structures on extensive grounds. The one that looked like the house was at the end of a long driveway leading up from the street.

He put on an undershirt, knowing he'd arrive sweaty, and after pulling on his backpack and locking up the house, he was soon coasting down the hill to the boulevard, then carrying his bicycle down the stairs into the metro.

From the station in the Valley he rode mostly on the sidewalk, to stay out of traffic, until he got into the hills. He had to pull out his phone several times to make sure he was taking the right streets. The higher he got, the narrower the roads were, but mercifully there were fewer cars. They still moved fast, careening around corners and brushing past his elbows, even though he was hugging the side of the road as he pedaled, breathing hard and sweating profusely.

When he was just a few dozen yards from the Whitby driveway, the gate he'd seen in the street photos already in sight, a black sedan with dark tinted windows roared up from behind him, passing inches from his handlebars, moving alarmingly fast. The driver braked at the gate, which had rolled open, and went through, negotiating the turn at only slightly reduced speed, then gunning it up the driveway.

The gate had closed again by the time Mason got to it. On the ivy-covered wall to one side, weathered metal lettering announced CLEMENTINE MANOR. He wondered whether naming the house was pure affectation or if anyone actually called it that. He pressed the button on a little intercom box in front of the gate, mounted at driver's window height. A woman with a Spanish accent answered, "May I help you?"

"My name is Braithwaite," he said, leaning closer. "I'm here for Margaret Whitby."

"You work for Anna?" the tinny voice asked.

"That's me."

"Come on up," she said. "Park in front of the left garage door."

She clearly didn't have an eye on him, if she thought he'd need a parking spot. He waited for the gate to retract a few feet and then mounted his pedals, pushing through the gap and up the driveway. The house soon came into view, built of heavy stone with tall windows on two floors, stately and fronting a courtyard that would have filled a city block in Mason's neighborhood. It had probably been ostentatious when it was built, maybe before the war, he estimated, but today it seemed almost modest compared to some of the monstrosities in these hills.

The black sedan was parked in front of the garage, off to the left of the house, and as Mason rounded the last curve in the driveway he saw a woman in a flowy dress step out of the front passenger's seat, a broad smile on her face. The car had been sitting there for at least as long as it had taken him to pedal up from the gate; why was she just getting out now? She walked toward the front door of the house, still beaming to herself, and either didn't notice Mason or chose to ignore him, her stride confident and unconcerned. She exuded the air of money, but she didn't look much like Cyrus—in the old photos he was a fair-haired white guy, and this woman was dark, with expensively coiffed African hair. It didn't mean she wasn't a Whitby, but she didn't carry herself like an employee either.

The driver's door opened, and a lanky man with pronounced cheekbones and oily blond hair climbed out. He stood with his hand on the car door, watching her walk into the house, his gaze intent. This was definitely an employee, in a black uniform to match the vehicle. He climbed back into the car and pulled it into one of the garage bays, the door rolling down behind him.

Mason thought about leaning his bicycle against the hedge in front of the house, but that would probably mar someone's view, and it might get moved by a gardener. Instead he leaned it against the garage, not far from where he'd been instructed to park, not bothering to lock it, and walked toward the house. The front door stood ajar, so he stepped inside, finding himself alone in the foyer. His entire house could have fit inside this space, but it wasn't opulent or flashy, paneled in old-school dark wood, the floor a checkerboard of black and white tiles.

A woman entered from the back of the house, her hair in a tight bun. Unlike the uniformed driver, she was dressed in a casual polo shirt and pants.

"Mr. Wrathway?" she said, and he recognized her voice from the intercom.

"It's Braithwaite," he said, pronouncing it carefully.

"Of course." She didn't correct herself, but flashed him a polite smile. "I'm the housekeeper. If you could wait for just a moment." Before he could ask her name she turned and trotted up the wide staircase to the second floor, and he was alone again.

It was quiet here, he realized, like the countryside, with no streets or neighbors close enough to be heard. Several sets of doors led off the foyer, all firmly closed, and a hallway disappeared under the staircase, where the housekeeper had appeared from. Straight back he could see through to a garden, lush and green and shady. He took a few steps toward it, thinking he'd take a look outside, but then thought better of it.

Instead he closed his eyes and tried to tune in to the house, quieting his thoughts and opening his mind. Clementine Manor, he thought, focusing on the name. He waited for insight to seep in from the fringes of his awareness. The only impression that came was something about its bulk—the house was imposing and established, far from ephemeral, but also constitutionally inert, not in any way dark or threatening. Hearing the housekeeper treading down the stairs again, he opened his eyes and turned toward her.

"Do forgive me," she said, with an apologetic frown, and continued past him to one of the doors near the front, knocking gently and then stepping inside, closing it behind her.

Mason sighed and turned to look outside again. Maybe he would go have a look at that garden, he thought, but then suddenly a man in a business suit burst from the room the housekeeper had entered. He strode out into the foyer, eyeing Mason over his glasses and scowling suspiciously. He looked to be in his forties, trim, with graying hair and clean-shaven, exuding an aura of old money.

"Henry Whitby," he said, enunciating carefully.

"The scion," Mason said.

Henry's eyes narrowed. "I guess that's accurate. And you are?"

Mason introduced himself, and Henry nodded.

"If you'd come into my office, Mr. Braithwaite."

"Call me Mason," he said, following him back toward the doorway, where the housekeeper waited, hands folded behind her back.

"Do you drink coffee?" Henry asked.

"I live for it."

"Rosalía, if you wouldn't mind," he said, pronouncing her name with authentic clipped Spanish vowels, and stepped past her.

"How do you take it?" she asked Mason.

"Just black. I'd love some water too," Mason said, and she nodded before she walked away.

Henry's office looked more like a library, as large as the foyer but with a lower ceiling, carpeted and lined with tidy bookshelves. A quartet of wing chairs sat alone in the middle of the floor, and at the far end were a desk and a credenza with more chairs, a little office island in the grand room. The windows beyond didn't look out on the garden he'd seen, but rather a sparse little wood with several towering eucalyptus trees.

It was a beautiful room, calm and inviting. Gesturing to the wing chairs, Henry bellowed "Sit"—too loudly, considering Mason was standing right in front of him. Mason dropped into a chair, grinning at the bluster, and Henry took an adjacent one, absently hiking up his pant legs to preserve the crease as he sat. It was a little odd that he was wearing a suit on Sunday.

"Unfortunately, Mother's not available," he said, meeting Mason's eye.

"Is that her decision, or yours?"

Henry frowned. "Hers. Not that it concerns you."

"I thought she had an appointment today with Anna."

"She's not feeling well," he said, watching Mason closely as he spoke. "However, she asked me to inquire as to how you might be able to help in this matter, and to ask about your rates."

Mason fished a business card out of his pants pocket and handed it to him. "First, I'd interview your guest to assess whether or not he's telling the truth. Then I'd do whatever research is necessary to confirm his claims or disprove them."

Henry raised his eyebrows. "That sounds pragmatic. I assumed you'd be a believer, hawking some arcane divination technique, calculating Mother's *I Ching* bubble quotient by the light of the waxing moon."

"I'm an investigator, not a showman, Mr. Whitby."

"It's just Henry," he said, his bluster fading. He glanced at the business card and read Mason's job title. "'Psychic investigator.' So what kind of investigating?"

Henry seemed like a practical guy, and Mason spun it that way. "Like I said, interviews, among other techniques, none of which require an audience. Research is about getting to the truth, and in my work I've found that people never tell the whole truth about anything. Once I figure it out, though, I can drag it into the open. It doesn't make everyone happy, but things tend to mesh together in the most satisfying way."

"I see."

"If it's easier, you can just think of me as a researcher. Look past the 'psychic' part."

"That's certainly more palatable," Henry said, "but how does being psychic play into it?"

"It's about insight. Background information that nudges me toward the facts."

He watched Mason for a moment, calculating. "I made the wrong assumption about what kind of person Anna was going to refer Mother to. What would it cost?"

"I charge five hundred a day plus expenses. For a job like this I'd ask her to hire me for a week. If I didn't have any answers by then, we'd reassess."

"What kind of expenses?"

"If I have to go out of town, or pay gratuities to obtain information," Mason said, gesturing vaguely.

Henry nodded. "That's fine. The most important thing to me is privacy. None of this can become news."

"I have experience dealing with the media. I call them in when I need their attention, but otherwise everything I find is confidential."

"Would you sign a nondisclosure agreement to that effect?" he asked, eyeing Mason closely.

"How many pages is it?"

"Just one."

"Then yes, without hesitation."

"Good answer."

There was a knock on the door, and Rosalía came in carrying a tray with a silver coffee pot, dainty porcelain cups, and a glass of water for Mason. Henry watched curiously as Mason guzzled the water while Rosalía poured their coffee. He thanked her as she left.

Once the door had closed, Henry sat forward. "Let's get started today. You seem like a reasonable person, and I'd like this cleared up as soon as possible." Henry rose from his chair. "Paperwork first."

He walked over and sat at his desk, sliding open a drawer and riffling through it, pulling out a folder. Studying Mason's business card again, he copied from it in rapid pen strokes, then looked up and waved Mason over.

Mason crossed the Persian carpet to the office space, dropping his backpack in one of the chairs facing Henry's desk and sitting in the other. Henry slid a page to him across the vast expanse of his desktop. Mason read through it quickly. It was basic legal boilerplate, only a few paragraphs, and Henry had already written Mason's name in the appropriate blank.

"It's pretty standard," Henry said.

"I'm not worried," Mason said, looking up at him. "I know it's just business."

He signed the form and sent it back across to Henry, who pulled a new manila folder out of his drawer and wrote Mason's name on the tab in block letters, slipping the page inside. Mason had

to smile; it was just the way he did things himself. Henry then stood and reached across the desk,
handing Mason a business card that bore only his
first name and a phone number.

"That's my personal cell," he said. "So you can
contact me directly."

"More important, I think, is that I talk to Mrs.
Whitby."

Henry looked confused. "She has passed on to
her greater reward."

Mason frowned. "When? You talked like she
was still alive when I walked in here."

Henry sank back in his chair and sighed. "Mrs.
Whitby was my wife. She died. Mother is just
Mother. Everyone calls her Margaret."

"I see—I didn't mean to upset you."

"You haven't," Henry said firmly. "Mother is a
very sensitive person, and not especially stable. If
she said she can't have visitors today, that's that—
it'll have to be another day."

"Perhaps you can fill me in on what you know."
Mason reached for his backpack and pulled out his
notepad.

"Let's go back to the comfortable chairs,"
Henry said. "I barely touched my coffee, and I feel
like I have to shout at you from here."

"That is quite the desk." It was almost too
broad to be practical, but he had to admit it fit the
scale of the room.

When they were seated again, Henry tented his
fingers and looked up at the windows.

"My great grandfather had a brother who lived in Spain," he began.

"Your great grandfather was Cyrus, correct?" Mason asked.

"Impressive," Henry said, meeting his eye. "You've done some research."

"Just the basics. I know he was a bootlegger, but it seems he wasn't a gangster."

Henry frowned. "We've been legitimate businesspeople since the end of prohibition."

Mason glanced around the room at the antique furnishings, the ornate bookcases. "If you say so."

"You're certainly not afraid of candor."

"As I said before, the truth tends to thrive in the bright light of day," he said, raising his eyebrows.

"Well, setting aside your doubts about my family," Henry said, "the brother in Spain was in manufacturing, but that side of the family's fortunes declined after the war. My father was always suspicious of their politics. He said they were mixed up with some disreputable people—the fascists—and so he didn't maintain connections with them."

"I see," Mason said, scribbling notes.

"In any case, even though we weren't in touch with them, we were aware of the Spanish relatives, and cousin Manuel, sadly childless, the last in the lineage."

"What was his surname?"

"Whitby," Henry said emphatically. "We're all Whitbys. Anyway, Manuel contacted Mother not long ago, in the winter, and they planned for him to visit Los Angeles. It was the first we'd heard from him in decades. Mother was very excited, as she doesn't have much of a social life outside this house."

"She's shy," Mason said, glancing up.

"Exactly. And Manuel showed up, as scheduled—but he's not Manuel. His name is Etor, and he's very confused. He's also much younger than Manuel would have been—Manuel was older than Mother."

"Why did Margaret believe this guy was an alternate version of Manuel?"

"Well, he had a letter from Mother, for one. I've seen it, and it's in her handwriting. She knows she wrote it to Manuel, but it's addressed to Etor."

"That's certainly intriguing," Mason said, writing it all down as quickly as he could.

"You can see why Mother sought assistance."

"I'm going to need to see that letter," he said, half to himself, and then looked up at Henry. "Is it possible Margaret could have a bit of dementia? Maybe she forgot who she wrote to."

He shook his head. "I discussed Manuel's visit with her several times before he arrived. It was definitely always about Manuel—in family lore and in Mother's letters."

"Do you have photos of Manuel?"

"Not as an adult. There are baby pictures of him somewhere, from when Cyrus visited Spain in the thirties. That's tangential, in any case, because Etor is a completely different person. The parallel-world story is quite convenient in that regard—he doesn't have to look like anyone in the family, and performing a DNA test would be pointless."

Mason nodded, writing furiously. "Anna said something about a passport."

"It's from a country that doesn't exist. The name escapes me, but you can look at it. He showed us on a map where it was supposed to be, and it's approximately where Andorra is, but it's not Andorra. He was confused by the map, and didn't recognize Germany. He had another name for Ireland as well, and he said New Zealand was in the wrong place."

"Did he actually say that he's from a parallel world?"

Henry thought for a moment. "Mother is the one who came up with that," he said finally. "She cooked up the idea with your friend Anna."

"When did he get here?"

"Thursday, and Anna was here Friday morning. She was quick to thrust herself into the middle of it. I know she's a charlatan, by the way," Henry said.

"Anna?"

"It's not possible to talk to the dead."

"I've seen her work, and I know she's an accomplished psychic," Mason said. "Margaret obviously believes that too."

"Mother is too impressionable."

"Anna works hard. What do you do for your money, Henry?"

He scowled, his face reddening.

"Seriously, though," Mason said. "Does Margaret

control the family money, or do you?"

"Why does that matter?" he demanded.

"I want to know whether it's possible for someone to con Margaret without your knowledge or permission."

"Right," he said, calmer now. "Margaret controls her own finances, not connected to the family business. Her assets are extensive."

"So if you think Anna is a fraud, can I assume you're not buying Etor's story either?"

Henry sighed. "More significant than my opinion is that Mother seems to believe it."

Mason scrawled on his pad for a minute, then looked up. Henry had a peculiar look in his eye, watching him with a faint smirk. Mason had seen that look before, and he knew what it meant, although he hadn't expected it from this guy.

Mason met his eye. "So when did your wife die?"

Henry looked startled, his grin vanishing. "Four years ago. It was a difficult age for our daughter. She was seventeen."

"But you're still single. Why is that? You're a good-looking guy—you'd have a lot of options." He held Henry's gaze. He'd never been good at flirting, but he didn't really need to be; the drive for connection was innate in most people. He wasn't even trying very hard, but he got a reaction—color rose in Henry's face and he looked away, shifting uncomfortably in his chair.

"I guess because my life can't look the way I

want it to," Henry said finally.

Mason wanted to ask him what that meant, exactly, but the door swung open and the woman he'd seen earlier, stepping out of the sedan, walked into the room.

"Daddy," she said, striding across the carpet, focused on Henry.

"Mason, this is Deborah," Henry said, twisting around in his chair.

"Hello," Mason said, rising from his chair.

"Don't get up," Deborah said.

"This is my little girl," Henry said, beaming at her over his glasses.

She climbed onto Henry's lap and put her arms around his neck, kissing him on the cheek. Sinking back into his chair, Mason was startled at the intimacy. Maybe she was younger than she looked. He glanced at his notepad and counted in his head. She had to be at least twenty-one.

"We were just talking about Etor," Henry said. "Mason is going to interview him."

"Etor's lovely," she said, turning toward Mason but keeping a firm grip on Henry's neck.

"Why do you say that?" Mason asked, smiling politely.

She frowned. "Because he is."

"Besides that, what's your sense of him?"

"Well, he's definitely a relative, despite what Father thinks."

"How would you know that?" Henry asked gently.

"I've been upstairs with him all morning. He told me everything about his branch of the family."

Mason had seen her arrive by car not long ago, so that was a lie. Was she protecting Etor, or herself?

"What did he say about his family?" Mason asked.

"Ask him yourself," she said impatiently.

"I saw your driver earlier," Mason said. "The blond. What's his name?"

"Eddy," Henry said, looking confused at the seeming non sequitur, but Deborah's eyes grew wide, locked on Mason.

"Perhaps you could show Mason up to Etor's rooms, and introduce them," Henry said.

"No, Daddy," she whined, disengaging from him and rising, pouting like a small child. Without another word she was gone.

"If you'll come with me," Henry said, watching her go but unfazed by her behavior. He stood, waiting for Mason to stuff his notepad into his backpack.

Mason followed him up the stairs, miming his deliberate pace. At the top, wide hallways stretched off into the house in opposite directions. Henry turned left, and rapped sharply on one of the first doors. Without waiting for a response, he pushed it open. Mason had expected to find a bedroom, but it was bigger than that. They were in a vacant sitting room, with doors at both sides leading to other rooms. Through the one that stood ajar, Mason could see a dressing table with a mirror. Margaret's long-lost cousin had his own suite.

Momentarily the door on the other side opened, and a dark-haired man stepped out. So this was Etor, the man from another world. He was nothing like Henry or Cyrus, with their ruler-straight noses and long, refined fingers. This guy was a mass of muscle, squat and thick, his hair slicked back like Deborah's driver. It looked better on Etor, though, more polished. He was about Henry's age and wore a sport coat, and shifted his gaze apprehensively from Henry to Mason.

"Etor, this is Mason Braithwaite," Henry said.

Mason glanced at Henry, flattered that he remembered his name, and how to pronounce it.

"Mason, Etor Yakobe," Henry continued. "Etor, Mr. Braithwaite is going to ask you some questions to see if we can't sort out this mystery."

Etor made a little bow from the neck. "Pleased to meet you, sir." His accent was slight, vaguely Spanish or maybe French.

"Call me Mason."

"Then you must call me Etor," he said, moving closer.

"I'll leave you to it, then," Henry said, eyeing Mason, and then walked out, leaving the door open.

"Shall we sit?" Etor asked, gesturing toward the sofa, his movements formal, distinctly foreign.

"What kind of name is Etor?" Mason asked, sitting on the sofa and dropping his backpack between his feet.

"It's Grapalian," he said, easing into an adjacent chair. "But you and Henry are pronouncing it wrong. The *e* is short, just one sound, not stretched out like your Saxon vowels. The *o* as well, it's just 'o.'"

Mason tried again, evoking high-school Spanish and the sound of Ned chatting with his grandparents. "*Etor.*"

"That's not too bad," he said, grinning appreciatively.

"Tell me about your home," Mason said, reaching down to pull out his notepad and quickly flipping to a fresh page. "What did you call it?"

"Grapalia."

"What's Grapalia like?"

"It's in the mountains, so we ski in winter when it snows, and go hiking in summer. There are a lot of banks—Grapalia is something of a money sanctuary."

"A tax haven?"

"That's the correct word," Etor said, nodding.

"It's in Spain?" Mason asked, jotting notes but watching Etor, only occasionally glancing down at his pad.

"Next to Spain, although Cousin Henry's maps don't show it." His brow furrowed. "All this has been very distressing. I feel like I don't have a home to return to."

"I can understand that. I assume you've searched for it online?"

"Yes," he said emphatically. "It's simply gone.

Like it fell off the face of the earth."

"Can I see your passport?"

Etor rose, wordlessly stepping into the bedroom. Mason pulled out his phone and opened the camera, turning off the flash and holding it down in his lap, but aiming the lens at the doorway. When Etor appeared he surreptitiously snapped a photo of him, pretending he was reading something on the screen, then distractedly set the device face down on the cushion beside him.

Etor's eyes narrowed as he sat, but if he'd noticed that Mason photographed him, he didn't say anything about it. He handed the passport to Mason.

It was burgundy and clothbound, reminiscent of other foreign passports he'd seen, the cover embossed with UNIÓN EUROPEA, then PRINCIPADO DE GRAPALIA. Below that was a crown surmounting an ornate shield and rampant lions, and at the bottom a decorative scroll with the phrase SANGUINEM ET PANEM.

"Is this Latin?" Mason asked.

"The motto of my country," he said. "Blood and Bread."

"Grapalia was part of the Roman Empire?"

"Of course it was."

"So you know ancient Rome, but not Germany or France."

"France, I know. I live a few kilometers from the French border. The other one I don't know. In my world, Berlin is in Austria, not ..."

"Germany."

Etor nodded.

"Is this country different now than in your memory?"

"I'd never been to Los Angeles," he said, pronouncing it the Spanish way, the *g* a breathy *h* sound. "But I'm not aware of any differences."

Mason opened the passport, turning it sideways to scan the identity page, with Etor's name and photo, his place of birth listed as simply "Grapalia." A few pages in was a lone immigration stamp from LAX, dated three days ago.

"You don't have a visa," Mason said. "Just an entry stamp?"

"Grapalia is part of the EU. We don't need a visa to enter your country."

"But they stamped your passport at LAX, even though it's from a nonexistent country."

"It's not nonexistent to me," he said emphatically. "I've tried to determine exactly when the … change happened, and I'm certain it was after the airport. I remember the immigration officer said something like 'I don't get many people from Grapalia.' So he knew my country. But when I went to a bank to change euros into dollars, it requires paperwork, and they didn't recognize my passport. Eventually they just wrote 'Spain' on the forms because the document is written in Spanish. I was changing a sizeable sum, and I suspect they didn't want to miss out on the commission. At the time I assumed it was sheer ignorance of my little homeland."

"What bank did you go to?"

"Zurich Bevorzugt."

"Can you spell that?" Mason asked.

Etor sighed in frustration but rattled it off as Mason wrote it down. "It's near the airport. Many wealthy Europeans use it."

"What about the money you got there? Can I see it?"

He stepped into the bedroom again and returned with a handful of cash bundles—still bearing the yellow bank bands, labeled "$10,000"—and handed them to Mason.

"There's fifty grand here," Mason said in amazement. "That's a lot of dough for a vacation."

"I live well," Etor said simply.

"Can I take a few of the bills? I'll return them."

Etor scowled. "You want to check whether they're counterfeit."

"Well, maybe I can determine whether it's from this world or from yours."

"Take it," he said, folding his arms.

Mason pulled three hundreds from the middle of one of the stacks, folding them and stuffing them in his pants pocket.

"I don't know why Cousin Henry doesn't believe me," Etor said. "I've been completely honest with him."

"Well, you have to admit, it's a pretty bizarre story." Mason watched Etor for a moment, assessing him. "Did you bring credit cards?"

Etor reached into his pocket and pulled out

a little silver clip that held several cards, handing them to Mason. They each had the familiar magnetic stripe, and on the front the gold-colored chip contacts, with the label BANCO GRAPALÉS and a stylized bird-shaped logo.

"I don't suppose you've tried to use them?" Mason asked.

"They wouldn't work. The bank doesn't exist. I checked online."

"What about other accounts?" he asked. "Email, that kind of thing?"

"Gone. All gone. The websites either aren't there, or my credentials are unknown." His face contorted as he struggled to keep it together. "I feel like I'm all alone."

Mason nodded. His desperation seemed sincere.

"Did I really fall out of my world?" Etor said.

"Do you think that's what happened?"

"I don't know."

"I know there's more going on all around than any of us are aware of."

Etor nodded glumly. "What's next for me?"

"I'm going to do some research," Mason said. "Are you spending much time with Margaret?"

"We've spoken. She's delightful, and sympathetic to my plight."

"Can I see the letter she wrote you?"

He brought it from the bedroom, a sheaf of onion-skin paper covered in looping handwriting and folded in thirds. "Dearest Etor," it began, "We would be most delighted to host you while you're in California." Scanning through the paragraphs, what she'd written dealt mostly with Etor's planned visit. On the last page it was signed "Margaret."

"Did Margaret recognize the letter?" Mason asked. Even though Henry had already told him that she had, he wanted to know if the answer would be the same.

"She said it was her handwriting," Etor said.

Mason nodded. He wanted to photograph it, but decided not to bother. The document had already been verified by its author, and it didn't mention anything that implied it came from elsewhere—except the word *Etor*.

Folding the letter, he gave it back, then pulled a copy of his business card out of his pocket and handed it to Etor.

"I'll swing by again in a day or two," Mason said. "Call me if you want to talk about anything."

Etor glanced at the card distractedly and set it on the arm of the chair with the letter.

"I don't know what you could possibly do to help me," he said. "I don't know how I got here, and I don't know how to get back."

"Let's see what we can figure out," Mason said, and rose, briefly placing his palm on Etor's shoulder.

He closed the door on his way out and went down the stairs, checking the photo he'd taken on his phone. It was a good likeness of Etor, showing his full face, even though he was squinting a little. He could crop it into a headshot later.

The door to Henry's cavernous office stood open, so he stepped inside.

"What did you think of the man from another world?" Henry called from his desk.

Mason walked over, waiting until he was closer before he spoke. "Grapalia. The man from Grapalia."

"Right." Henry laced his fingers behind his head and leaned back in his chair.

"It's certainly an intriguing story," Mason said, standing in front of his desk.

"Are you convinced?"

"I'm going to reserve judgment until I know more."

"Well, I'm not buying it," Henry said. "I didn't want to tell you that until you'd talked to him yourself, because I didn't want to bias you. To me it's beyond reason that he tumbled into my house from some other dimension."

"You sound like my boyfriend," Mason said. "If you can't explain it using lab equipment, it doesn't exist."

Henry grinned, his eyes bright. "What's he like, your boyfriend?"

"He's a great guy, although he tends to disbelieve anything paranormal."

"He sounds well grounded."

"Or maybe blinkered by the mainstream," Mason said, raising his eyebrows. "In any case, the passport was weird. I took some of his cash so I can check whether it's bogus or not."

"Good idea."

"I still need to talk to Margaret at some point. She might have other insights."

"When you've done some of your research, I'm sure she'll be curious to hear your thoughts."

"Maybe I'll stop by tomorrow."

"That's fine," Henry said. "Do you need some money up front?"

Mason shook his head. "We can figure that out later." Despite his bluster and skepticism, Henry didn't seem like the kind of guy who would stiff him.

He said good-bye and walked toward the door, feeling Henry's eyes on him the entire way. In the foyer he met the housekeeper, just coming down the stairs.

"Rosalía," he said, stopping her before she disappeared into the back of the house. "Do you work with Margaret?"

"Sometimes," she said, her eyes wary.

"Does she come downstairs for meals, or does she always stay in her room?"

Rosalía frowned. "She eats upstairs."

"Is she bedridden?"

"Not at all. Why are you asking?"

"I'm doing some research for Henry, and I wanted to talk to her."

"Not today," she said, shaking her head.

"I understand that she's a nervous person. Is she under a doctor's care?"

"Listen, Mr. ..."

"Mason."

"Mr. Mason. I have work to do," Rosalía said firmly. "You can see yourself out."

He watched her walk into the back of the house, then turned and went out into the court-yard, past the heavy front door, still propped wide open. Rosalía probably wanted to let the breeze into the house. The spring weather was still mild, and there would be no security concerns up here inside a gated yard.

Strolling toward the garage, he saw the driver, Eddy, standing near his bicycle, hands on his hips, staring at it.

"That's my ride," Mason called to him.

Eddy whirled around and pulled the cigarette from his lips, concealing it in his hand. "I wondered what that was doing here. No one ever comes up on a bicycle."

"I did," Mason said cheerfully.

He looked Mason over, from his shoes upward. "You don't look like Mr. Whitby's usual guests."

"You're his driver?" Mason asked.

"Might be," Eddy said, his tone guarded, suspicion in his eyes. He dropped the cigarette and crushed it into the gravel with his toe.

Mason frowned. "You clearly work here. I saw you driving the car."

"A smart guy, huh? What do you want with me?" he demanded.

"Nothing," Mason said calmly. "I'm doing some work for Margaret. Do you know her very well?"

"I don't know anything," he said, gesturing wildly. "I drive the cars. Yes sir, no sir, get paid. That's all I know."

"Funny you put it that way," Mason said. "Deborah seemed quite happy when you two got home earlier."

For an instant fear flickered in Eddy's eyes, quickly replaced by anger. "You ought to keep your nose out of other's people's business," he said, his voice low. "Otherwise it might get broken."

"No offense," Mason said, holding up his palms. He didn't find Eddy particularly intimidating, but he didn't want to provoke him either.

Eddy turned on his heel and disappeared into the garage.

When he was out of sight Mason stepped over and looked down at the cigarette butt. Eddy had palmed it like it had been something illicit, so Mason had assumed it was pot—a big no-no for a commercial driver. But stooping to look at it, it wasn't that. Among the smooth pebbles, the crushed remains showed the distinctive brown shreds of regular tobacco. He didn't want to touch it, but there was a brand stamped on the filter. Looking around to make sure he wasn't being observed, he picked up an oblong stone and poked at it until he could read the name: Gitanes.

Once he was partway down the driveway and out of sight of the garage, Mason stopped and pulled off his backpack, fishing out his pad to add some notes:

Eddy: driver
evasive, angry
claims not to know anything about Whitbys
smokes Gitanes

He thought for a moment, then added:

some connection to Deborah.

Three

The ride down out of the hills and back to civilization was much easier than riding up, and Mason enjoyed coasting where he could, the breeze in his hair. When he got to the metro he decided to cycle just a little farther to the NoHo arts district, where he knew a decent little vegan place to grab a falafel and a coffee.

Afterward he wheeled his bike onto the train and rode all the way downtown, emerging into the daylight again near the central library. Locking up his bicycle, he walked through the green space in front of the library and into the art deco temple to knowledge, admiring the pyramid that capped the grand structure. He walked down the escalators into the depths, settling into a desk and connecting to the library's catalog with his computer.

There was nothing about Grapalia, as expected, nor did it come up in a general Web search. Etor's name was similarly missing, but when he looked for resources on parallel worlds, he found an overwhelming amount of information. He spent an hour just parsing the source material, eventually locating several books that held promise. After he'd written down the call numbers he folded up his laptop and stuffed it into his backpack, then went upstairs to the relevant stacks. Soon he was parked at another desk with a small pile of texts.

Etor wasn't the first person to step through from a different version of this world. In the nineteenth century a man had shown up in Germany, claiming to be from a nonexistent country called Laxaria. In Paris in the early twentieth century a man speaking an unknown language explained that he came from Lizbia. The authors documenting the cases provided a range of possible explanations—Lizbia was a mangled rendering of Lisbon, even though the man didn't speak Portuguese, or possibly Lesbos, although he wasn't Greek either. One writer speculated that in a time before mental health care, the man from Laxaria suffered from undiagnosed delusional disorder. But neither that nor any of the other explanations were adequate to explain all the details of the cases, Mason thought. Perhaps Etor was just the latest traveler in a disbelieved but well-documented phenomenon.

Picking up another book, he read about a case in Japan, after the war, when a traveler arrived at Haneda Airport with a passport from a nonexistent country. He had been detained but disappeared from his room overnight, never to be seen again. Reading through the case, he could feel his heart pound faster at the similarities to Etor's story. The man's passport said he was from Taured, a small country in the Pyrenees between Spain and France. He seemed confused that the Japanese officials had never heard of his homeland.

The author explained that careful research showed no trace of the story in Japanese newspapers, and no mention of it in the West prior to its publication in a paranormal magazine in the 1960s. The logical conclusion was that the whole thing had been made up by the magazine writer. Mason set the book aside and sat for a minute, lost in thought. The fact that a story so similar to Etor's was almost certainly fictional implied that Etor's story was phony too. But some part of him found it so tantalizing, wanted to believe it. The older stories were harder to discount. Original sources were obscured by the passage of time, and they'd never been definitively researched. But he knew that didn't make them true.

Pulling out his computer, he logged into the library's newspaper index and looked for mentions of Margaret. She had lived most of her life well below the radar, mentioned only in lists of party guests or banquet attendees. Henry's father came up more often, in articles about the family business and the charitable foundation, but he'd left Margaret a widow more than a decade ago, after which point her name never again made the news. It fit with what Henry had told him, and what Rosalía had said: Margaret had become a recluse.

Some of the search results pointed to print sources that were dated before things had been digitized, but it didn't seem worth the effort to hunt through spools of microfilm for long-ago mentions of Cyrus and his lineage that would almost certainly turn out to be just as spurious as the newer references that he could click to and read on his screen.

Henry's activities hadn't been very newsworthy either, except in tragedy. Mason clicked on several articles from local media that documented the dramatic death of his wife. She had tumbled from the roof of a parking structure, and none of the reporting provided any explanation beyond a lone guarded mention that she was "rumored to suffer from depression." One article mentioned Deborah, although not by name, as her only child. Another called her the "wife of local financier Henry Whitby." That seemed like a grandiose title for what Henry did, which seemed to be little more than tending a bunch of investments, but maybe there was more to Henry's career than that.

Looking for subsequent stories on Henry's wife revealed nothing, and no matter how he phrased the search, he couldn't find a single mention of her cause of death. He pushed the machine away and slumped in his chair, frustrated. It didn't make any sense that no media outlet had followed up when the coroner's report was released. But someone with Henry Whitby's resources could easily throw his weight around to keep news about his wife's suicide out of the media. It had to be that, he realized. If there had been a homicide investigation, even Whitby-scale money couldn't have kept that out of the news.

Maybe some gossipy unofficial source had more to say about his wife's death than the media did. On the Web he dug around for other leads on Henry. Scanning dozens of pages brought up the same worthless snippets, repeated verbatim on blogs and news aggregators. Clicking on a deeply buried search result finally led to a fresh story, a short puff piece about the Whitbys' charitable foundation paying for upgrades to a sports arena. The photo showed Henry in a crowd of a dozen people, glad-handing a sleazy local politician, everybody grinning like eight-year-olds about to get birthday cake. It was dated a few years ago, and Henry looked the same, although perhaps there was a little less gray in his hair. The caption read "Brother Whitby consigning the funds for the upgrade."

Why would the trustees of the sports arena call him "Brother"? He thought about it. The most likely explanation meant that he was going to have to drop by Rugley Hall.

Folding his computer closed and stuffing it into his backpack, he walked up to street level and out into the library's little park, where he found an open spot on a bench and pulled out his phone, swiping through to the end of his contact list and dialing.

"Yoshida," a familiar voice answered.

"I'm glad I caught you," Mason said. "Are you at Rugley Hall today?"

"I'm actually headed there now. I should be in my office in an hour."

"Do you mind if I drop by for a few minutes?"

"Welcoming your visit is implicit in laying out my schedule to you," Yoshida said.

Mason laughed. "I'll see you there."

He walked across the street and got a double espresso, savoring it as he sat at a table on the sidewalk, watching the traffic and the pedestrians, thinking through everything he'd just read. Eventually he unlocked his bicycle and descended into the metro. He was feeling worn out, but there was more to do, and Rugley Hall was almost on the way home.

Mason had done some work for Yoshida, and he'd spent time at Rugley Hall. The building had started life mainly as a Masonic meeting house, but as membership in the fraternal order dwindled over the decades, its role had shifted to that of a de facto community center. In his role administering the hall, Yoshida was involved in both sets of activities.

Cycling up to the building, he admired its pleasant redbrick facade, surmounted by a Masonic motto, ORDO AB CHAO, engraved along the top, just below the gently peaked Roman roof. "Order from chaos." This place was indeed an island of stability in a chaotic metropolis, and even though the Freemasons probably had a mystical meaning in mind when they employed the phrase, it always rang true to Mason, much more than the neon in Anna's storefront ever would—a validation of what he did for a living, literally writ large. It was one reason he liked coming here—that, and the fact that he was party to some of the secrets lurking behind these walls, the altruism and public service of Yoshida and his peers that stretched from the mundane into the metaphysical realm.

Walking through the front doors, he nodded to the guard posted at the desk, then made his way to Yoshida's office. The door was open, and Yoshida stood to greet him when he stepped in.

"It's good to see you," Yoshida said, smiling broadly and waving for him to sit. He was rail-thin, probably in his sixties, and unfailingly formal—a smile was the warmest display of emotion Mason had ever seen from him.

"You too," Mason said, dropping his backpack between his feet as he sat in front of his desk. "So what can you tell me about a Freemason named Henry Whitby?"

"Nothing," Yoshida said flatly.

"Because you don't know him?"

"I can't gossip about lodge members. If you were a Freemason, I could, but you're not."

"So he's in your lodge."

Yoshida smiled. "I can't tell you that. Did his

name come up in one of your cases?"

"So you want me to give you information, but you don't want to provide any," Mason said, raising his eyebrows. "It seems we find ourselves at an impasse."

Yoshida snorted and shook his head. "Without confirming his affiliation with any organization, I know Henry Whitby personally, and I can vouch for his character."

"Cool," Mason said, surprised. They might have known each other in the business world, but it was much more likely that his hunch was valid— Henry was a Freemason. "I think you're probably right that he's on the level. I didn't get any hinky vibes from him."

"So you've met," Yoshida said, raising his eyebrows.

"I'm doing some work for him."

"I see."

Mason was thankful he didn't ask for details. That was the upside to Yoshida refusing to gossip: there was no pressure on Mason to break his own promise of confidentiality to Henry.

"Do you know what happened to his wife?" Mason asked.

"That was tragic. I know it was hard on Henry."

"Was it a suicide?"

"I don't know any more than what was in the papers."

"Right. It's probably not relevant anyway."

They chatted for a few minutes, mostly about

the non-Masonic goings-on at Rugley Hall, and then Mason stood and excused himself.

"Always a pleasure to see you," Yoshida said as he left.

Mason rode through the leafy neighborhood to his own, and when he walked inside, he saw Ned out on the balcony, his nose in a book. When he stepped out through the French doors he found Peggy too, lounging at the other end, wearing a floppy hat, sunglasses, and denim shorts, her legs exposed to the late-afternoon sun.

"Working on your tan?" Mason asked her.

"Just getting some base color. I barely see the sun on weekdays."

"So did you locate the missing planet?" Ned asked, setting his book down.

Mason chuckled and stooped to kiss him hello, then sat between them on one of the patio chairs. "I actually signed an NDA, so I'm not sure I can talk about it."

"Those are just so you don't sell it to the media," Peggy said. "Who are we going to tell?"

"Nobody would believe it anyway," Ned added, putting his feet up on the balcony railing.

"As long as you don't phone it in to channel 10," Mason said, and told them about his visit to Clementine Manor.

"You didn't talk to the matriarch?" Ned asked.

"Not yet."

"I thought she was the one who called you in. What's her name?"

"Margaret. I'm told she's a little sensitive. Hopefully I'll meet her tomorrow."

"That kind of money lets people insulate themselves," Peggy said. "It's a shame, because they get stuck, and stop striving. Being a little hungry can be a great motivator."

"I don't know if she's insulating, or if she's just a really delicate person."

"I'm sure Margaret puts her bra on one breast at a time, just like everybody else," Peggy said.

"Thanks for that image," Ned said wryly.

Mason frowned. "I don't get what that's supposed to mean."

Peggy pulled down her sunglasses to meet his eye. "It means don't be blinded by the money into thinking she's unique. The same standards apply to her as to everyone else. If you need to talk to her, push your way in."

"That's probably good advice," Mason said.

"What about the cousin from another planet?" Ned asked. "Did he have three arms, or green skin?"

"He's just an ordinary European type—polite, dressy. He was at a loss as to why this happened to him. Henry is actually more interesting than the interloper. I asked him why he was single and he said, 'My life can't look the way I want it to.'"

"He sounds closeted," Ned said. "If his social life is about boardrooms and country clubs, I'm sure he's expected to marry a woman and produce heirs."

"And then marry a string of increasingly younger women," Peggy added.

"He definitely set off my gaydar," Mason said. "Henry was married to a woman, but she died. Their daughter is in her twenties but she acts like a four-year-old around him."

Ned frowned, meeting Mason's eye. "Make sure you keep your wits about you up there."

Ned made a stir-fry for dinner, and afterward Mason went into the office they shared and sat at his desk, taking his laptop and notepad out of his backpack. From his bottom drawer he pulled out the manila folder with his earlier notes from Anna and wrote THE MAN FROM GRAPALIA on the tab. After he read through the pages he'd written today, he tore them off and slid them into the folder, then pulled up the photo he'd taken of Etor and cropped it, brightened it a little, and sent it to Ned's printer, slipping the copy into the file as well.

Next he dug around in his pants pocket. Henry's card was there, and he punched the details into the contact list on his phone before dropping the card in the file. More compelling were Etor's hundred-dollar bills. He smoothed them out on his desktop, turning on his banker's lamp to get a better look at them. Online, he looked up how to determine a bill's authenticity, and all three of them passed inspection—the color-shifting ink changed from green to brown the way it was supposed to, and the shiny foil ribbon showed the expected 3-D effect. He'd double-check at a bank tomorrow, but from what he could see these were real.

Climbing into bed, Mason was grateful to be horizontal after such a long day. He lay there for a moment, eyes closed, rapidly sinking toward the hypnagogic state. But Ned climbed on top of him, playfully drumming his fists on Mason's chest.

"Are you on hormone supplements or something?" Mason asked. "You're so damn randy."

"I know you're tired. Maybe we can just make out for a minute."

It was a bait-and-switch strategy, because they both knew they wouldn't be able to stop once they got started. He pulled Ned down and kissed him.

Funny that Henry had wanted to know what kind of guy Ned was. Mason had told him Ned was a skeptic, but Henry probably wanted to know what he looked like, what his personality was like.

He pulled away from Ned for a second, and ran his fingers through his thick hair.

"You OK?" Ned asked.

"Of course," he said, but really he was wondering why he was thinking about Henry right now.

Hours later he dreamed he was looking at himself in a mirror, intently studying his features. The image pulled him up toward consciousness, until he was lying there awake. It was still dark out, but he felt drawn to the floor mirror, so he forced himself to get up and went over to it, heart pounding. His reflection was vivid, almost surreal, and even though it followed his movements precisely, like a mirror image should, it felt different—brighter than it ought to be, electrically charged.

Closing his eyes, he stood there for a minute, inducing an altered state of mind. It was a technique he'd learned recently called hidden mind, and it was the easiest way to access the reflection as a separate entity. It felt like being thinned out, his mind diffusing into the space around his head. He focused on the idea, dispersing his consciousness, and when he finally opened his eyes he was calmer, even a little spacey. It was instantly clear that it had worked—his reflection wasn't a mirror image anymore, standing there watching Mason, hands on his hips.

"You woke me up again, didn't you," Mason said.

"So are you going to make me whole?"

"What would be the purpose of that?"

"I'm not sure yet," his reflection said, biting his lip. "It's something about the Whitbys. I think you're going to need my help." He grinned luridly. "That Henry sure is a looker, huh."

"Not really my type."

"Dude—I live in your head, remember? I know you're attracted to him."

"That sounds like something subconscious," Mason said, gesturing vaguely. "He's a client. My feelings about him are strictly professional."

"Sure they are. Wouldn't you just love to pull him onto your lap, professionally speaking, and smell his hair? Pull his glasses off, and feel his skin? Find out whether there's any trace of stubble, any imperfection on that pretty face?"

"Jesus, man, I'm with him," Mason said, jabbing a finger toward the bed, trying to keep his voice down.

"If you weren't exclusive with the brunette, though, Henry would be a lot of fun."

"Is that why you woke me up? To dig through my subconscious?"

"Actually I wanted to explain how to get me out of the mirror."

Mason sighed.

"You'll need two other people who have some psychic chops," his reflection said. "Not Hanh, she's too weird. Maybe the tarot woman."

"Anna."

"Whatever. And the old *nagual* who was on Gilbert's roof during the Penstock Canyon thing, or Peggy's boyfriend. The three of you have to get into the vivid awareness state. Do you know what that is?"

"Never heard of it."

"You tell yourself you're going to be sensitive to expanded information about the physical world. More colors, more sounds. Everything gets supersaturated. Then you all focus on the reflection, and direct your energy into it, and I'll be able to step through."

"Does it have to be this mirror?"

"No, but it should be a big one—you're a big dude. Water works too, but we'd both get wet, and who wants to be squatting around a damn swimming pool? Let's just use a mirror."

"OK," Mason said.

"Can you remember all that?"

"I'll remember," Mason said, even though he had no intention of doing any of it.

Four

Slapping his alarm off, his first thought was irritation at his shrink, Miss Cassie, for scheduling his session so early. She knew he wasn't a morning person and yet she always did this. He made coffee, then ate some fruit, staring into space as he munched, gradually waking up. His reflection, he remembered. It had seemed like a bizarre idea last night, pulling him out of the mirror, but thinking about it now in the sober light of day, it was starting to make more sense.

After he got dressed, he went into the office to kiss Ned good-bye before pulling his bicycle out of the garage and heading down the hill to the metro. By the time he surfaced across from Miss Cassie's office, his resentment of her had faded. He loved coming here, craning his neck to take in the soaring art deco tower, and she had a knack for keeping him focused, even though she questioned so much of what he did workwise.

The building's glammy facade belied the starkly modern offices inside, gut-renovated to expose the concrete and brick. He rode up in the elevator, knocked on her door, then pushed it open. Miss Cassie waved him in, and he took his usual spot, on the sofa by the tall windows that looked out over the Financial District. She soon joined him, settling into her chair and folding open her tablet.

She read through her notes for a few seconds and then said, "How was your week?"

"So why would a grown woman act like a four-year-old with her dad?" he asked, and described Deborah climbing onto Henry's lap, cuddling with him despite him being in the middle of a meeting.

"Did that make you uncomfortable?" she asked.

"Let's not make this about me."

Miss Cassie laughed. "Are these people that you know well, or acquaintances?"

"I just met them. They're clients. I'm trying to understand them."

"What you saw might be their established pattern. It's not necessarily dysfunctional or unhealthy. How old is the daughter?"

"About twenty-one."

"It sounds like she rebonded with him after the teenage separation."

"How do you know she separated from him?"

"Everyone does," she said, raising her eyebrows, "or should. Do you remember being embarrassed by your parents and wanting to avoid them when you were a teenager? It's a natural phase, so that you can become an independent adult. It sounds like this young woman just isn't embarrassed by her father anymore."

"I guess it didn't seem unhealthy, just odd," he said.

"Speaking of the parental bond, we've talked about your primary caregiver a little," Miss Cassie said, swiping through her notes.

"We have. My mother."

"What was she like when you were very young?"

"It's hard to remember."

"Was she in tune with your feelings?" she asked, glancing up but still digging back through her notes. "Or did she ignore them?"

"It was a long time ago," Mason said irritably.

Miss Cassie spent a moment reading, then looked up. "Still, it's important. Your anxiety stems from that imperfect connection."

"Even though I can't even remember it?" he demanded.

She nodded.

"Well, that sucks."

"It doesn't mean you can't be healthy now," she said gently. "You're not at the mercy of your past."

"I never thought I was. Until right now."

She smiled. "It gives us some ground to cover."

They talked about it, and before he knew it their fifty-minute hour was up. Riding down in the elevator, Mason felt queasy, worried he'd been pre-programmed to be fearful, and irritated that he was just figuring that out.

He left his bicycle parked and walked half a block to a bank, waiting in line and then stepping up and greeting the teller behind the window.

"Can you tell me if these are counterfeit?" he asked, digging Etor's hundreds out of his pocket.

"Before I check them," the teller said, looking him in the eye, "you should know that if they are, I'll have to confiscate them."

"I'm pretty sure they're legit," he said, sliding them under.

She looked the bills over carefully, holding them up to the light and then passing them under a device that looked like a hole punch with a purple bulb in it.

"They look real to me," she said finally, slipping them back under the window. "The holograms are all there, and the UV light shows the right colors."

"Thanks," he said, stuffing them back in his pants pocket.

Outside, he stopped for a quick espresso and then unlocked his bicycle, carrying it down into the metro and standing with it on the train out to the Valley. He had plenty of time to think on the long bike ride up into the hills. Pushing aside his disquieting chat with Miss Cassie, he focused on the matter at hand. Technically Margaret was his primary client, so hopefully he'd be able to talk to her today—if he could get past Rosalía.

Panting and sweaty, he rolled up to the gate at Clementine Manor and pressed the button on the intercom. When Rosalía answered he gave his name.

"Mr. Whitby is not in," she said.

"I'm here to see Margaret."

She didn't respond right away, but eventually the tinny voice said, "Come on up. Do you remember where to park?"

"I do," he said, and waited for the gate to slide open. It was a revealing question—if she thought he was in a car, it meant that she hadn't compared notes with the driver, Eddy.

There were no vehicles in the courtyard as he pedaled up, and the garage doors were all down. He parked his bike around the side of the building, hopefully out of Eddy's view, if he was around and feeling aggressive like yesterday, and walked across the gravel to the house, where the front door was again propped open. Inside, he waited, admiring the chandelier hanging high in the foyer, myriad chunks of glass suspended in the air and sparkling in the golden light. It must have been there yesterday, but he noticed it now because it was illuminated. It had to weigh a ton.

Rosalía appeared on the stairs, trotting down to greet him.

"I'm so sorry, but Margaret isn't feeling well," she said. "She can't have visitors today."

"What about Etor, is he around?"

"He is, but I think it's his nap time."

"He's having a nap? Like a toddler?" he asked, putting his hands on his hips.

"He's European. They do things differently."

"Like sleeping in the middle of the day?"

"You could wait for him in the ballroom, if you'd like."

"Maybe I'll bother you for a glass of water."

"Of course. The ballroom is through there." She pointed to a doorway opposite Henry's office.

"Can I just come to the kitchen with you?"

Suspicion flashed in her eyes, but she said, "Sure."

"Do the Whitbys throw a lot of balls in the ballroom?" he asked, following her under the stairs.

"Sometimes," she said cautiously, not looking at him.

The kitchen was large and outfitted more like a restaurant than a home, an industrial vent hood over the range, a long counter forming an island down the middle of the space, an array of pots and utensils hanging from a rack above it. At the far end a doorway led outside—through the glass in the doors he could see that inviting back garden. Rosalía poured him a glass of water from a pitcher in the fridge and set it on the island. While he drank, she took a paring knife from the wooden block on the island and sat on a stool nearby, peeling potatoes into the sink, ignoring him.

"So what do you think of Etor?" he asked.

She shrugged, not looking up from her task. "He's just another house guest."

"Does he spend a lot of time with Margaret?"

"Yes."

"How much time?"

"A few hours this morning." She grabbed another potato and looked up at him. "They seem intimate. Like old friends."

"Why does she see him and not other visitors?"

"He's family, Mr. Mason. It's different."

"It's just Mason." He stepped to the fridge and opened it, refilling his glass from the pitcher inside, then turned back to her.

"Have you been in the room when they're talking?" he asked.

Rosalía frowned. "Why are you asking all these questions?"

"I'm looking for deception."

"Deception is part of life. It's everywhere."

"Even in this house?"

"Even here," she said.

"Like what?"

She glanced toward the entrance. "It's not my place to say. Everyone has secrets."

"Who do you distrust the most in the house?"

"Eddy," she said, without hesitation. "He's lying."

"About what?"

"Everything."

"How well do you know him?" Mason asked.

"Listen, are you finished with your water?"

"Of course," he said, smiling and holding up his palms. "Before I go, though, did you know Henry's wife? I heard she fell off a building."

Her hands froze in mid-cut, almost imperceptibly briefly. "Mr. Whitby has had a difficult time since then. It was painful for all of us."

"Did she have depression?"

"I have work to do," she said, her tone sharp now.

"Right. I'll get out of your hair."

He walked back into the foyer, waiting for a moment to make sure Rosalía didn't follow him, and then walked up the staircase, as quietly as he could, rolling his feet stealthily, heel to toe, the way he'd learned the samurai did. He stopped at the top and listened to the house. It was quiet.

Etor's door was closed. He walked over and stood next to it, listening, but there was no sound from within. He tried to visualize the weight of the door, what it had felt like yesterday, whether it was heavy and soundproofed or thin and light, but he couldn't remember.

Farther down the hall another door hung open. He walked over to it and looked in. It was a mirror image of Etor's suite, with the bedroom out of sight in the back, and blandly decorated, like a hotel room. It had to be another set of guest rooms. It looked completely unlived-in, quiet and empty, so he stepped inside, looking around the space, then strode over to the bedroom door and peered in. It was similarly generic, with a print of watercolor roses on the wall, a dark wooden vanity with nothing on it, the carpet carefully vacuumed. But someone had been sleeping here—a pair of jeans were draped over the easy chair, a folded magazine on the bedside table, and on the bed a laptop, left open, its screen black. Glass doors to a balcony looked out on the gravel courtyard, the garage to one side, the trees beyond.

He thought about sliding open the doors and walking out onto the balcony, but he hesitated. This was clearly someone's space. In that moment a voice came from behind him, nearly stopping his heart.

"What are you doing in my room?"

He whirled around. It was Deborah, just walking into the sitting room, looking more bemused than angry.

"You're the one Daddy hired to interview Etor," she said, a spark of recognition in her eyes.

Mason felt the color rising to his cheeks, but he stuck his chin out. "You seem to think he's telling the truth."

She scoffed. "Etor? I don't know whether he is or not. I don't really care."

Mason frowned. "You told your father he was a great guy."

"I may have been yanking Daddy's chain," she said, a smirk playing on her lips. "And you haven't answered me. What are you doing in here?"

"I was looking to talk to Margaret."

"Well, she's not in here, obviously. If she didn't

agree to see you, you can't see her. Don't go snooping around."

"Right. I'm sorry to have troubled you," he said, and stepped quickly past her, back into the hallway.

Either that wasn't really her room, or she had the personality of a robot and had decorated it accordingly. No, he decided, it was a smokescreen. She was hiding something behind all that blandness.

Etor was standing in his doorway now, eyeing Mason as he approached. Had he overheard them?

"How's it going?" Mason asked. "Do you have a minute? I have your money."

"Come in," Etor said, gesturing with a flourish, and went to the sofa.

Mason dropped into an adjacent chair, setting his backpack on the floor. The coffee table was cluttered with detritus—a rumpled necktie, misfolded sections of a newspaper, a partly unwrapped granola bar with a bite out of it. But one item snagged his attention—a little blue box, cracked open to reveal that it was half full of cigarettes, and a wispy logo above the brand name: Gitanes.

"How was your siesta?" Mason asked.

"Restorative," Etor said pleasantly.

Mason nodded to the pack of cigarettes. "They let you smoke in here?"

"On the balcony."

"Your cash," Mason said, pulling it out of his pants and dropping it on the table. "It's real."

"I knew that," he said.

"So how much time are you spending with Margaret?"

Etor's face clouded. "What's that to you?"

"I'm trying to figure out how you got here."

"You think I'm a grifter," he said sharply. "That's what the question implies, that I'm trying to unduly influence Margaret. I'm hurt."

"It's unfortunate that you're so sensitive," Mason said, his eyes narrowing. "You have to admit, though, it's a pretty wild story. Have you ever heard of someone stepping through from another world?"

"I'm surprised you'd even question it, being a psychic. Other worlds must be your stock-in-trade, like Anna."

"You met Anna?"

"Briefly. Margaret told me about her."

"So you do spend time with Margaret."

"I see her," he said, struggling to keep his tone even. "We're cousins, and I'm her guest. Of course we speak."

"Are you planning any business ventures together?"

Etor stood abruptly. "Get out," he said, his voice low, but his chest was heaving with emotion.

"Sure," Mason said, rising and casually pulling his bag onto his shoulder. "We'll talk again real soon, Etor."

He walked toward the top of the stairs, not looking back. He hadn't intended to rattle the guy, but at least Etor had acknowledged that his bizarre story might raise suspicion that a scam was in the works, which paradoxically made that scenario seem less likely. But it wouldn't be hard to fake taking offense at Mason's insinuations, and overreacting was certainly an effective way to put an end to the questioning.

The quest for Margaret would have to wait—looking down into the foyer he saw Henry, standing just inside the front door, wearing a suit.

Henry looked up at Mason, surprised, and called to him in his booming business voice: "Mr. Braithwaite."

"It's just Mason, remember?" he said, descending the stairs.

"Of course. Force of habit. I'm not on a first-name basis with very many people."

That struck Mason as sad, but he didn't pursue it. "I was just having a word with Etor."

"Any progress?"

Rosalía appeared, and Henry handed her his briefcase, which she carried into his office.

Mason waited until she was gone, then glanced back up the stairs and spoke quietly. "Well, he's being cagey about his relationship with Margaret."

"That's distressing," Henry said. He pressed his lips together, thinking. "Can you stay for a few minutes? I'd like to see how he deals with you."

Henry hailed Rosalía as she stepped out of his office. "Could you ask Etor if he would come down and have coffee with us?"

"Of course," she said, and to Mason, "You take it black, correct?"

"Good memory," Mason said, nodding to her before she turned to go upstairs. He followed Henry into his office.

"Sit in that chair," Henry said, pointing to the one opposite his own, "so he has to sit between us."

It was a good idea, Mason realized—Etor would be positioned so that Henry and Mason could each observe his interactions.

Etor soon joined them, greeting Henry with warm words and his idiosyncratic little bow. His previous ire had apparently evaporated. Rosalía soon followed with the coffee, poured it for them, and then left again. Even though Henry had framed it as a chance for him to observe Etor responding to Mason, he did most of the talking himself.

"Mason is concerned about your relationship with Mother," he began, setting his cup on the table.

Etor bristled visibly. "Are you concerned about it?"

"I'm paying him to decide what I need to be concerned about."

Etor glanced at Mason, disdain in his eyes, but quickly masked it, turning back to Henry. "Margaret and I are getting acquainted. She doesn't have a lot of stamina, so it's just a few minutes a day." He sipped at his coffee and continued. "We're family, and we have the right to communicate. It's really none of your business, Henry. And by extension, nor is it the business of your proxy."

To Mason's surprise, Henry replied calmly,

sounding almost conciliatory. "I don't mean to offend you, Etor. You're being treated as a welcome guest, wouldn't you agree?"

Etor nodded.

"Still, this is my house, and I need clarity about what's going on under my roof."

"You know my story," Etor said intently. "I'm an open book. What other questions do you have? Please—ask them."

Henry looked at Mason expectantly.

"I need to do more research about the parallel worlds thing," Mason said, "and then I'd like to question you in depth. Can you set aside a few hours to do a thorough interview in the next day or two?"

"I have nothing but time. You know where to find me," he said.

"Thank you, Etor," Henry said firmly, and Etor rose from his chair, nodding to Henry and walking out.

"Good work, man," Mason said once he was gone.

"What do you mean? He didn't say anything, except to challenge my authority in my own house."

"He just agreed to be interrogated. He wouldn't have done that for me—I got in about three questions today before he shut me down."

"I see," Henry said, his expression softening. "I guess we make a good team."

"I'm going to hold him to it, and give him the full-on third degree."

Henry chuckled. "I should thank you for being my proxy, as Etor put it. I have to be more polite with him because of Mother."

"We'll definitely get to the bottom of this," Mason said, draining his coffee cup and rising.

Sneaking back upstairs to look for Margaret was out, because Henry accompanied him to the front door, his hand gently draped on Mason's shoulder as they walked, and then stood there watching Mason cross the courtyard to the garage. The look in his eye, the physical contact—he could feel Henry's interest in him, transcending the business relationship, seeping into the personal.

Henry had retreated from the doorway by the time Mason had retrieved his bicycle and looked back, but as he was climbing onto the pedals a car pulled around from behind the garage. It was a rag-top, low-slung and red, the engine throaty, and the top slowly folded back as the vehicle's tires crunched across the courtyard, heading for the driveway. He caught a brief glimpse of the back of the driver's head as it pulled away. A shock of blond hair—Eddy.

The car was out on the street and gone by the time Mason pedaled through the gate, but after he reached the first junction and turned onto a bigger street, he caught up to it. Even in the hills the afternoon traffic caused backups. He passed the long line of idling vehicles on the right, and was close to passing Eddy when the queue started moving again, gradually picking up speed. Before the convertible pulled away Mason got close enough to read the rear plate, and he worked to memorize the number. Trying to think of a mnemonic for the letters in it, ADG, he hit on *angry driver guy*. No way would he forget that.

Surprisingly, even just coasting downhill with gravity, he was able to keep pace with the traffic all the way into the Valley, not passing the ragtop but not losing sight of it, a slash of red ahead in the sea of automobiles. Maybe he'd even be able to follow Eddy, unless he got on the freeway. His interest in the guy had swelled significantly since he'd learned that he smoked the same obscure brand of ciggies as Etor. It could be that Eddy had simply bummed one off the interloper—or was there more to it?

Traffic sped up once he turned onto Lankershim Boulevard, and Eddy was soon gone. It wasn't a great loss, Mason decided. Shifting focus, he rode past the metro station, intent on getting something to eat in NoHo. But there was the convertible again, angry driver guy holding up traffic by backing into a meter space, right in the thick of the commercial district. He grinned at his good luck and stopped in the gutter, one foot on the curb, far enough back that Eddy wouldn't notice him. Eddy left the top down and got out to fiddle with the meter, then strolled up the sidewalk, away from Mason, languorously holding out his car key and locking the doors, not looking back. His stride was confident, even cocky, Mason thought. Something about the guy rubbed him the wrong way.

He pedaled past the convertible, trailing Eddy

at a safe distance, and stopped when Eddy ducked into an unmarked doorway. Locking his bike to a street sign, he pulled out his phone and stood at the curb, zooming in on a map of the street. The door Eddy had gone into was in the last building on the block, marked on the map as St. Mary of the Grove Church, but the front entrance was on the cross street, meaning Eddy had gone in the back. He hadn't walked in there like a man looking for Jesus—something else was going on. Mason was going to have to go in.

He paused to snap a picture of the front of the convertible, making sure the plate number was clear. As he pocketed his phone, a passerby shot him a suspicious look.

"Sweet ride, don't you think?" he said, flashing a smile before walking up the block toward St. Mary's.

The door Eddy had gone into was propped open, with a paper sign taped on it: MEETINGS, with a hand-drawn arrow pointing inside. All Mason could see inside was an empty service lobby with an elevator door and the top of a flight of stairs, everything painted brownish-pink. A woman with a denim jacket walked past him into the hallway and turned back.

"Are you looking for NA?"

"Oh—no, that's not my meeting. I must be in the wrong place."

She studied him for a second. "Emotions Anonymous, right? They meet here this evening. I think it's at seven."

"Thanks," he said, and watched her start down the stairs.

So Eddy was a recovering addict. He wanted to listen to that meeting, but there was no way to do that without sitting in, and if he did, Eddy would know he was being followed. Mason went back to his bike.

The "narcotics" part of Narcotics Anonymous was a pretty broad category, he thought. Eddy was skinny, like a lot of the tweakers floating around Los Angeles, but there were specific twelve-step groups just for meth. It was more likely opiates. Thinking about Eddy's demeanor, he could imagine the guy might have some existential pain he wanted to obliterate.

A few blocks away he found a coffeehouse, and went in and ordered an espresso and three vegan oatmeal cookies, then found a table in the crowded space. There was a band playing on the little stage at the back, just two women, young enough that they might even be teenagers, both playing guitars and belting out an upbeat ballad. They were polished, and glammed up, and knew how to work the room, catching everyone's eye.

He thought about Peggy as he watched them, munching on his cookies. These two were so unlike her, working a busy café in the middle of the day, but they were ready for the mass market. Peggy could easily look like these two, if she wanted to, and she could perform that kind of music, breezy and accessible. But she didn't. She'd never be a superstar, he realized. But knowing her, she was probably content with that.

He pulled out his phone, found Henry's number, and sent a text.

What's Eddy the driver's last name?

Henry's terse reply came moments later:

Connolly. Why?

Mason smiled at that and typed a quick response.

Doing some research.

Next he texted Matt, Peggy's boyfriend, asking if he had time to get together. He didn't have to wait long for a reply.

Home from school after 5. Meeting Peggy. Join us for dinner?

Even though his full-time work was teaching, Matt dabbled in the psychic field and had collaborated with Mason on past cases. Mason texted back and got the name of the place to meet, then texted Ned to ask if he wanted to come downtown to join them. Ned answered soon after:

Thanks, but I'll use the evening for some me time. Enjoy.

Finishing his espresso, Mason watched the band wrap up their set, then headed out to the street to unlock his wheels. The red ragtop was still parked on the boulevard as he rode by, and he glanced into the seats, but they were empty.

Forty minutes later he was cycling in the Arts District, once a warren of century-old warehouses repurposed into studio spaces by artists, these days displaced by upscale housing, shops, and restaurants. "You know the gentrification of a neighborhood is complete," Matt had told him, "when a high-end supermarket opens," and sure enough, there it was, stands of ripe fruit and leafy vegetables pushed out on the sidewalk, a calculated throwback to the days when food didn't come from a factory and there weren't sixty thousand homeless people living on the streets.

He found the restaurant and locked up his bike. Inside he found Peggy and Matt at a table, both still dressed for work, Peggy in a gray suit and Matt wearing a vest and a colorful necktie, the knot loosened, top button undone. Mason smiled as he walked up, seeing that Peggy had her hand on Matt's back, massaging in a slow circle.

He greeted Peggy with an air kiss and pulled out the chair across from them. Matt was clean-shaven for a change, probably because he'd been working, his brown mane neatly combed.

"No kisses for me?" Matt said as Mason sat down.

"I could plant one on you, if that's what you

really want."

"Nah, man, I haven't been vaccinated for rabies. So what the fuck is so important that you'd interrupt our date?"

"Is that what this is?" Peggy asked, eyeing him askance. "If so, you're buying."

"Work," Mason said. "Would you be willing to help me and Anna pull my doppelgänger out of a mirror?"

"Meaning there'd be a physical copy of you running around the city?"

"That's the idea."

"Sounds like bad news for the city," Matt said. "How much work is it?"

Peggy looked shocked. "Wait a minute," she asked Mason. "Why would you do that?"

"I'm not sure, exactly," he said. "He wants out, and he says that he can help me."

"Mason, that's insane," she said emphatically.

"Not really. He's just me, right, or some part of my mind. I have to trust that my subconscious knows best."

The waiter stopped by, and Mason ordered a couple of veggie tapas. He waited for Peggy and Matt to order, then explained the procedure his reflection had outlined.

"If you think it's safe, sure—I'll help," Matt said finally.

"I'm usually down with all your psychic stuff," Peggy said. "This just seems like ... beyond."

"I still have to ask Anna," Mason said, "but

why not see if it works?"

Their food came, and after he'd started in, he asked Matt, "What do you know about detecting deception?"

"I work with college students, so I'd say a lot. There are many iterations of 'My dog ate my homework.' Is it for the mirror séance thing?"

"Different issue. I have to interview a guy who claims he's from another reality. Peggy knows the scoop. He's already taken a disliking to me, but I thought maybe I could bring you in as an objective third party. You could grill him and see if you think he's on the level, and we could compare notes."

"Why Matt?" Peggy asked, twirling pasta around her fork. "It sounds like you need a cop, not a biologist."

"I figured he's kind of a no-nonsense guy," Mason said, eyeing her. He knew Matt had no qualms about being aggressive—acting demanding was second nature to him. Looking to Matt, he added, "I can pay you."

"How much?"

"How much do you want? It'd be a few hours' work."

"I have no idea. Maybe three hundred bucks?" He looked to Peggy for input, but she just shrugged.

"That works," Mason said. "Can you spare some time this week?"

"I don't teach on Wednesday, and I can move my office hours around." Matt took a bite of string bean, lost in thought. "I'll look into interrogation techniques. I can't slap him around, though, right?"

"I pity the man from another world," Peggy said.

After they'd eaten, Mason said good night and rode to the metro, eventually wheeling his bike into the garage as night was falling. Ned was stretched out on the couch with his tablet.

"Hey, sweets," he said, looking up. "How was your day?"

"Great," Mason said, dropping his backpack by the front door and sinking onto the sofa at Ned's feet. "I chased a sports car."

Ned chuckled. "On your bike? What kind of car?"

"A red convertible. I have a picture of it," he said, pulling out his phone, finding the photo he'd taken of Eddy's front license plate, and passing it to Ned.

"It's a Mustang," Ned said. "See the horse in the grill?"

"Are they expensive?"

"Not really."

"So it wouldn't be weird to see someone on a basic salary driving one?"

"The way credit and car leases work, it wouldn't be weird to see a homeless person driving one. Half the people in this town drive cars way above their pay grade, but they don't actually own them."

It made sense—Eddy's ride didn't reflect his income, only his aspirations.

He told Ned about Eddy, and following him

to the twelve-step meeting. "What do you know about NA?" he asked, gently massaging Ned's toes. "Is it the same vibe as AA?"

"The underlying issues are the same, but I'd say NA people are more hard-core."

"Meaning what?"

"Alcoholics are closer to the mainstream. With NA, they're already doing something illegal, so they're less inhibited about how far they go on the way to rock bottom. Mostly that just means stealing stuff. Street drugs are way more expensive than booze."

"What about Emotions Anonymous?"

"That's like AA too, but instead of alcohol messing up your life, your emotions are."

"So it's for people with all the drama, who catastrophize everything."

"Exactly."

Mason scoffed. "This woman at the NA meeting assumed I was looking for the EA meeting. Is that what I present to the world every day? 'I'm an emotional wreck'?"

"You know, that program might be really helpful for you," Ned said, deadpan. "Would you like me to check whether they meet in our neighborhood?"

"I'm already heavily invested in Miss Cassie," Mason said, smiling at his dry humor. "No room for more head-shrinking."

"Speaking of crazy, how about an episode of *Pica Confessions*? I saw a preview—this guy eats blackboard chalk. They don't use it in schools anymore, so he has to source it from Eastern Europe."

"That does sound mesmerizing," Mason said, and they spent an hour with the cringe-inducing diversion before bed.

Late in the night, fast asleep, he dreamed about standing in front of the floor mirror. He didn't physically get up to go stare into it, at least he didn't think he did, but as he stood there, his reflection glowered impatiently, waiting for him to focus. "Let's go," he said insistently, and clapped his hands.

Five

Waking up when his body told him to, for a change, Mason relaxed on the balcony with a mug of espresso, munching on berries. Once the caffeine had rendered him sufficiently lucid, he pulled out his phone and called Anna.

"You must have news," she said as she picked up.

"Something like that. Can I swing by your shop today?"

"Any time," she said, "but I'll be busier later on."

He went inside and found Ned in the kitchen, heating up a tortilla.

"Burritos for lunch?" Mason asked.

"That's the plan. My mom sent those beans you like."

"Set me up, then—I'll join you." He climbed onto a stool at the counter.

"I thought you just ate breakfast," Ned said as he pulled out another tortilla.

"Why would that stop me from having lunch?"

Stomach full, Mason pulled on his backpack and descended the hill. It was depressingly gray out, as it was for two months or so every year. No one called it spring, because spring was the few weeks of warm-up right after the winter rains; this was LA's fifth season: May gray and June gloom, to be followed immediately by the heat of summer. Usually the marine layer would burn off sometime in the afternoon, the pattern mimicking Mason's daily arc from groggy to attentive.

After he'd changed trains downtown, he was soon in Anna's neighborhood, locking up his bike and pulling on her shop door. A handwritten sign was clipped to the heavy curtain into the next room: WITH A CLIENT. He settled in to one of the chairs in the front of the shop to wait.

Checking his phone for messages, he realized he could overhear Anna's session. Her voice was clear, but the client's was softer, muffled, impossible to parse.

"What it means is that one of your obstacles is your limiting beliefs," Anna said. "You think you can't get the job, but you can. You need to believe that you can."

Mason had to smile. It sounded more like a psych session than a psychic reading.

Eventually the client left, following Anna through the heavy curtains, thanking her, and stepping out into the street. He didn't even notice Mason, sitting in the corner beyond the glare of the neon window sign.

Once she'd closed the front door, Anna asked, "How are things going with Margaret?"

"I haven't even met her yet," he said, rising from his chair and picking up his backpack.

Anna looked concerned. "I know she has issues. Come on back."

Mason followed her through the consult room, its round table still dramatically spotlighted, and back into the office, where she poured him a mugful of acrid liquid from the ancient coffeemaker. Once she'd taken the other chair, he told her in broad strokes what had happened at Clementine Manor.

"I've only briefly met Henry," she said. "I don't know Deborah or Eddy at all. Margaret is reclusive, but part of my work has been encouraging her to get out of that room."

"There's something else," Mason said. "Can you me help me conjure someone? I think it'll be simpler than the time we did it for Hanh."

"Probably," she said, raising her eyebrows. "Who?"

"My reflection wants out."

"Are you sure that's safe?"

Mason rubbed his chin, wondering if he should reconsider. "What do you think?"

"It depends," she said. "Do you trust your id?"

"Is it meant to be trusted?" He thought about what Miss Cassie had brought up the day before, his imperfect childhood attachment. If his reflection represented that unknown part of his mind, there was a lot going on there. "He seems to have information that I don't have," he said finally.

"Of course. He's from your subconscious." She smiled. "It's not unheard of, but if you bring him here, just be prepared."

"I'd like to try."

"Then let's do it. It's work, so I'll need to get paid. I can give you a professional discount. How does four hundred sound?"

"I can do that."

"Good," she said, absently twirling a pen on the desktop. "I don't have a mirror, so you'll have to bring one. Do you have a third psychic?"

"Matt, the guy we conjured for Hanh."

"The lost boy who didn't bathe?" she said, surprised. "He struck me as a bit reckless."

"I think he's learned from that experience. He's a lot cleaner these days too."

She nodded. "My last client is at nine, so let's start at ten."

"Tonight?" Mason said. "That seems fast."

"You said he wants out. If you're going to do it, why wait?"

"Good point," he said. "I'll check with Matt."

She rose, and he quickly drained his coffee, setting the cup in her little office sink.

"I hope you can work things out for Margaret," Anna said, seeing him to the door.

"Me too," he said, and waved good-bye.

On the street he unlocked his bicycle and straddled it for a minute, pulling out his phone to text Matt.

Does tonight work for the mirror séance?

His reply came soon after:

Fuck yeah.

Matt drove an SUV, which would make transporting the mirror easier. Mason wrote back:

Swing by after dinner. We have to pick up supplies.

Sliding his phone into his pants, he took a deep breath and started pedaling. Ready or not, this was really happening.

It didn't take long to get to the central library, and he locked his wheels to a rack along the sidewalk before descending into the structure. Beyond Etor's claims and the other stories of people who had stepped between worlds, he wanted to read about the many-worlds theory, the serious physics that Ned had talked about.

Lots had been published about it, and he spent some time digging through articles in periodicals that explained the science for nonphysicists. It wasn't anything new, but it arose from quantum physics, which to Mason was a counterintuitive jumble that was hard to conceptualize. Some critics of the many-worlds theory said it wasn't even scientific, because it was impossible to test or observe, which made it a philosophical notion. Nothing in the scientific reporting said anything about overlaps or breaches between worlds. Once reality splits, the thinking went, the various layers—each independent universe—were forever discrete, evolving on their own and not affected by the others.

A broader search for anecdotal experiences of the many-worlds theory led Mason to a lengthy cascade of Web posts from people who theorized that they had somehow skipped between recently bifurcated versions of reality. A common theme was near-miss car crashes: an impending collision that was certain to be fatal but left no injury, no scratches on the vehicles, leading to the assumption that the experiencer had shifted to another timeline. The key difference from Etor's story was that these people thought they'd shifted at the moment of the collision, just as the timelines branched, so their memories were consistent with the past. Etor claimed to have switched worlds sometime after they had split, perhaps decades or centuries, based on the differences he'd described.

Eventually he'd read enough about the science, and the anecdotal themes that kept repeating themselves. He sat back in his chair. Logically, it made little sense that Etor had arrived here from

Grapalia, when universes more recently split from our own were absolutely discrete and unreachable.

Shifting gears, he connected to the county's criminal records database and searched for Eddy. Cases in other jurisdictions wouldn't show up here, he knew, but he needn't have worried; there was a long list of records for Edward Connolly. There was no photo of him to confirm that it was Henry's driver, but the birth date provided fit with Eddy's age, and the kind of crimes—mostly theft, and a burglary—seemed right for a former addict. He read through a couple of the court filings, which were slow going because of the esoteric legalese and arcane references. Eventually he figured out that most of the incidents weren't classed as felonies, and Eddy had done no jail time, somehow negotiating his way out of it on the felony burglary charge.

Rubbing his eyes, Mason sighed and folded his computer closed. He wasn't going to bother researching the plate number on the convertible, as he had plenty of information on the guy now. None of the crimes were violent, either, which was reassuring, and the most recent one was over four years ago. Maybe twelve-step was working out for Eddy.

Packing up his stuff, he headed back out to the street. The sun had finally burned through the gray, casting long late-afternoon shadows. As he stooped to unlock his bike, a man in a black suit and a fedora stepped out of a car that was parked at the curb with its blinkers on. It was a little unusual to see someone dressed like that, all in black, but the city was full of odd characters, and Mason wouldn't have looked twice if the guy hadn't made a beeline for him.

"Mr. Braithwaite, do you have a moment?" he said, his tone businesslike.

"Do I know you?" Mason straightened up, keys in one hand, the reassuring heft of his U-lock in the other.

"Not personally, but we know your work."

Mason frowned. "Who's we?" he asked, his fingers tightening around the lock. "And who are you?"

"My organization is handling the situation around the visitor from Grapalia," he said, his voice low. "We'd like to ask you to divest yourself."

"Why?"

"Things will go better for everyone if there's no interference."

Mason wasn't worried—there were other people around, strolling in and out of the library—but the man in the fedora was standing uncomfortably close.

"What organization do you represent?" Mason asked.

"I can't elaborate."

"Well, you're not the person who employed me, and since I don't see a gun or a badge, I'm going to have to say, pass."

The guy leaned closer. "Don't make me come after you again," he said tersely. "You'll regret it." Not waiting for a response, he turned and walked back to the car, climbing in and disappearing behind the dark tint of the windows. As the sedan pulled away, Mason stepped over to the curb to try to read the license plate, but there was only a blank black rectangle, not even a paper dealer tag. Taking a photo would have been a good idea, he realized, watching the car drive away, but it was too late.

His heart pounding, he went back to his bike and climbed on, pedaling toward the metro. Once before he'd met a mysterious man in a fedora, when he'd been working the Penstock Canyon case, but unlike that incident, nothing about this man was paranormal. Mason's instincts told him this was nothing more than an ordinary guy in a dark suit, driving a black car.

Once he was on the train he pulled out his notepad and recorded all the details he could remember: how tall the man was, his skin tone, his hair color, what kind of car it was. He hadn't seen the make, but it looked a lot like the car Eddy drove for the Whitbys.

As he thought about it, he realized it was possible that some three-letter government agency was aware of Etor's bizarre story, but if they truly wanted Mason to distance himself from it, they would have used force. Power takes action to achieve its goals; it doesn't issue vague threats in the hope of intimidation. No, this man in the fedora didn't represent real power. And Mason wasn't about to be dissuaded.

On the ride home he decided not to tell Ned about the encounter, needlessly stressing him out. A while after he got in, Ned made them dinner, Caesar salad and fried tempeh with plum sauce, and as they sat at the dining table, Mason told him in vague terms about his plan for the evening.

"What's the goal of the séance?" Ned asked.

"It's about getting in touch with part of my subconscious," he hedged.

"That sounds more like a job for your shrink," Ned said, munching on romaine lettuce.

"With any luck it'll enhance my psychotherapy."

"I can see the logic. When a house is completely engulfed in flames, you call in more than one fire truck."

Mason shot him a look. "At least I'm working on my stuff," he said. "Maybe you're the one who needs a meeting."

Ned laughed. "I'm not against mental health care. I'm just not in need of it right now."

"I think it's more of a regular maintenance kind of thing. Like flossing."

"I'm sure Miss Cassie loves that perspective," he said wryly.

Not long after they'd cleaned up, Matt rang the doorbell, and Mason went to let him in.

"Give me a second," Mason said, leaving him at the door and going into the office, pulling his top drawer all the way out. At the back he stashed some of the money from when he got paid in cash. He pulled out bills large and small until he had about seven hundred dollars, then pocketed it and slid the drawer shut.

Ned was chatting with Matt at the front door when he went back out.

"So where's your chick?" Ned asked.

"Fuck me—don't let her hear you call her that," he said. "I think she's rehearsing for Thursday."

Ned chuckled. "Do you know what the performance is about?"

"Not really. I think we're supposed to be wowed by the freshness of it, so she hasn't let any details slip. At least not to me."

"Us neither," Ned said.

"What about *your* chick?" Matt said, turning to Mason. "Is she ready?"

"Let's roll," Mason said, and kissed Ned good-bye.

"So where's the gear?" Matt asked as they walked out to his SUV.

"We need a big mirror," Mason said. "That thrift store on Sunset always has furniture. Let's try there."

They climbed into his car, and Matt navigated down the hill toward the boulevard, flicking on his headlights in the fading daylight.

"Have you ever heard of guys in black fedoras making veiled threats?" Mason asked. "In the paranormal world, I mean."

"Only as it relates to flying saucers, and even then it's mostly way back, like 1950s and 1960s."

"That's what I thought too."

"There's a book about it, called *They Knew Too Much about Flying Saucers*. One of the early

UFO researchers got so scared by hinky guys in a black suits that he quit the business."

"I didn't know you were a saucer-head," Mason said. "How cool is that?"

"I'm not, really," Matt said, stopping at a red light. "It's important stuff, though. Our cultural history."

"It happened to me today outside the library. One of them accosted me."

"A guy in a black fedora? No fucking way. What did he say?"

"He told me to stop investigating the man from Grapalia."

"Did he say who he represented?"

"He implied that he was from some official organization, but I don't think he was."

"He had a badge?"

"No badge, no ID, no gun. He didn't have the persona that cops have either, that air of authority. I wondered about one of the three-letter agencies."

"When the feds get embroiled in paranormal stuff, it's always the Navy. Did he have that kind of vibe, like a military guy?"

Mason thought about it. "Not really."

"So if he's not a cop or a fed, that part was bullshit."

"The other thing that doesn't fit is that there was absolutely nothing psychic about it. You know how you can feel it when it's in the air? Nada."

"It wasn't paranormal, then."

"That's what I'm thinking. He looked like he

came from central casting—the black suit, the black car."

"He probably did," Matt said emphatically. "There are lots of hungry actors in this town. Someone slipped him fifty bucks and told him 'Go intimidate copper-top over there.' Lots of people would jump at that gig."

"So the question," Mason said, ignoring the slur, "is who would pay an actor to play a character and try to threaten me?"

They pulled into the thrift store parking lot. Inside, Matt got sidetracked at a rack of men's shirts, flicking through the hangers.

"Could I wear this for work?" he called after Mason, holding up a blue plaid shirt that looked better suited to camping.

"Furniture," Mason said firmly, beckoning him onward.

The biggest mirror for sale was leaning against a dresser, tucked next to a sofa. Mason heaved it out to inspect it. Standing it on end, it was taller than he was. A length of wire was screwed into the back of the wooden frame so that it could be mounted horizontally on a wall. The wood was scratched and scuffed, but the glass was unmarred, and there were no flaws in the reflective coating.

"That's the right size," Matt said, finally catching up with him, the plaid shirt in hand.

"The sticker says thirty-five bucks. That seems like a lot for a banged-up wall mirror."

"You cheap bastard," Matt said. "Just buy the

damn thing."

Mason chuckled. "I guess I'd better."

They each picked up an end, Matt hanging the shirt on the mirror's mounting wire, and carried it to the register, setting it down against the counter. After Mason paid for it, Matt bought his shirt, then helped Mason carry the mirror out. It wasn't that heavy, but they walked slowly, Mason trying to coordinate his steps with Matt's confident pace. Matt balanced his end on his hip as he reached to open the back of his SUV, and the two of them slid it onto the carpeting inside, Matt pausing to flip down the backseat to make room to push it all the way in.

"Looking good," Matt said, slamming the lift gate down.

"You can even use it to try on your new shirt before we start the séance," Mason said.

Matt laughed, climbing in behind the wheel.

"So I asked a colleague of mine how to do an interrogation," Matt said, once he'd pulled out into the traffic on the boulevard. "She does a whole class on it. She says the Israelis actually use one-on-one interrogation at the airport instead of body scanners."

"A prof at Cal State?" Mason asked, incredulous. "What kind of faculty teaches interrogation?"

"Criminal justice and corrections. She just gave me a crash course, but I'm confident I'll be able to interview your guy."

"What does it involve?"

"Basically you keep asking questions and try to get the subject to contradict themselves. You can repeat details of their story, but with little changes, to see whether they correct you or not. You keep it moving fast, so they don't have too much time to think."

"It sounds intense," Mason said. "Do we need to record the session?"

"Detecting obfuscation all happens in the moment, so you don't really need to listen to it again later."

"Are you still up for interviewing my guy tomorrow?"

"Fuck, yeah," Matt said enthusiastically.

Mason grinned to himself in the darkness. Etor had no idea what he was in for.

With Mason's directions, Matt was soon pulling up in front of Anna's storefront. There were several open meter spaces, as most of the businesses on the block were shuttered at this hour. Mason climbed out and tried Anna's door; it was unlocked, and the little bell suspended above it jangled. Anna stepped out of the back.

"Where's the mirror?" she demanded.

"In the car," Mason said. "We'll bring it in."

Matt already had the back of the SUV open, and the two of them carried it inside, Anna trying to keep her ample bulk out of the way as she held up the curtain for them to bring it back into her consultation room. They set it down vertically, leaning against the wall.

"Beautiful," Anna said cheerfully, looking it over. "Should I Windex it?"

"It's fine," Matt said. "All the dust rubbed off in the back of my car."

Anna followed him out to the front, and once he'd closed up his SUV and come back inside, she locked the front door.

Back in the reading room, she scooped her crystal ball and its base from the table and set them gently in a corner.

"You'll need to see your whole reflection, no?" she asked Mason.

"I think we all have to be looking at it," he said.

"In that case, we should move the table out of the way," she said.

Matt helped Mason lift it aside, and then set three of the chairs facing the mirror. Anna turned the room lights way down.

"Atmospheric," Matt said.

"It's easier to concentrate," Anna explained. And to Mason, "You sit in the middle."

He complied, settling into the chair, looking uneasily at his reflection, tilted slightly because of the angle of the mirror against the wall, the floor in the reflected room sloping downward.

"Are you ready?" Matt asked, easing into the chair beside him.

"Oh, yeah. We haven't even done anything yet," Mason said, "but I can feel the energy, buzzing around my scalp."

"We're going to use vivid awareness, yes?" Anna

asked, taking her seat.

"That's the plan," Mason said. It was odd to be looking at them beside him in the mirror, rather than the usual configuration for such events, sitting in a circle. What a lineup they made. All three of them looked tired, rumpled, apprehensive.

"Can you explain vivid awareness for me?" Matt asked.

"You expand your conscious mind beyond your usual senses, to take more in," Anna said.

"That's the definition of every psychic technique I've ever used," he said flatly.

"You concentrate on getting additional information about physical objects in your surroundings, not the hidden world." She gestured to the mirror. "In this case, Mason's reflection. You'll see more depth in the shadows, new colors in the folds of his shirt."

"I haven't ever done it," Mason said, "but I've heard everything starts to look supersaturated."

"Exactly," Anna said. "Like a prolonged rush of blood to the head."

Mason could already feel it, even though he wasn't trying. He thought at first that it was just his eyes adjusting to the low light, but it was more than that, the shadows deepening, his perspective changing. His reflection was pushing him toward it, he realized, anxious to be brought into this world.

"When you reach that frame of mind," Anna continued, "both of you, say 'Come out,' and direct your energy to pulling the reflection out of the mirror."

"I'm ready," Matt said, and they all fell silent.

Mason saw the two of them relaxing as they shifted their focus, their eyes growing glassy. He tried to concentrate on his own image, clearing his mind and looking for changes. It took a while, but he focused intently, and the small enhancements he was seeing gradually expanded: the muddy brown fabric of his shirt erupting into an array of purples, oranges, and greens, shimmering with energy. His skin and hair too were vibrating, as if charged with electricity. The glass had become sharper, more than a mirror.

"Come out," Anna said softly, and a moment later Matt said the same thing.

Mason felt his heart pounding, not sure he was completely ready, but he focused on the image and murmured the phrase: "Come out."

His shirt was positively strobing now, moiré patterns flashing through it. He imagined reaching out, pulling his reflection toward him. He had the strangest sensation, the feeling that he was falling forward. But he hadn't moved—he knew he hadn't. It was his reflection, he realized, leaning ahead, then rising out of the chair. It was an alarming sight, but he held his focus, mentally drawing it toward him.

The reflection stepped over the mirror frame, ducking and twisting sideways to get through. He took a moment to regain his balance, then stood upright. It broke Mason's focus, and the vivid colors were gone. Weirdly, he could still see himself in the mirror, a third version, but once again an accurate mirror image, in ordinary colors, sitting there slack-jawed, a look of alarm on his face.

"Fuck me," Matt said softly.

Mason's doppelgänger stared at him intently, as stunned as Mason at this development.

Anna reached out slowly, her fingers brushing against his shirt cuff. He turned to her when he felt her touch, seizing her hand.

"I'm real, toots, if that's what you're worried about," the newcomer said.

"You're warm," Anna said, her eyes wide.

"He sounds just like you," Matt said slowly.

"It's weird, I know," he said, glancing at Matt but fixing his gaze on Mason. "It's weird for me too."

"What do we do now?" Mason asked, not breaking eye contact.

"I've got things to do," he said, putting his hands on his hips. "Can I borrow your bike? My keys won't fit. They're all mirror images of yours."

"What things?" Mason asked.

"Just things. We'll get all caught up later."

"He's not here," Mason said.

His doppelgänger frowned. "Who's not?"

"Wheels. He's at home in the garage. Matt drove me."

"Right," he said. "So no bicycle. Can I borrow a credit card?"

"Why?"

He sighed impatiently. "Because the ones in my pocket won't work—they're mirror images of yours. I won't do anything crazy, I promise. I need a phone, and some other stuff. I'll spend as little as possible."

Mason hesitated, glancing at Matt, whose eyes were locked on the newcomer.

"Give me the blue one," he said. "Your spending limit isn't very high on it anyway."

Mason pulled his wallet out of his pants and slipped the card out, wordlessly handing it over.

"Thanks," he said, and looking at the others in turn, "Thank you all for your help."

Anna murmured an acknowledgment, staring at him, mesmerized by the apparition.

"Now, don't freak out and cancel it on me," his doppelgänger admonished, slipping the card into his pants pocket and turning to leave.

"Where are you going?" Mason called after him.

"I'll be in touch," he said, and ducked through the curtained doorway. A moment later the front door lock clunked open, the little bell jangled, and he was gone.

"I should have had a plan for what to do with him," Mason said finally. "What was I thinking? I assumed we'd just hang out and talk."

"Obviously he has his own plans," Anna said, twisting sideways on her chair, her enthrallment evaporating.

Matt was lost in thought. "He's just like you, only more ..."

"Decisive, maybe?" Anna offered. "Persuasive?"

"What have I done?" Mason asked, avoiding his own gaze in the mirror.

"There's no point in questioning it now," Anna said, rising from her chair and patting him on the back. "It's done. You should be happy that we succeeded."

Matt looked up at her. "I'm still freaked out that it worked. What the fuck is he going to do?"

"He's part of me," Mason said, "so hopefully nothing crazier than I would do."

"He's not really from you, though, at least not your conscious mind," Anna said. "He's from your id."

"What the hell does that mean?" Matt demanded.

"It means you don't know what he's capable of," Anna said.

Mason gestured helplessly. "Should I be worried?"

"If he goes apeshit, cancel his fucking credit card," Matt said. "That'll slow him down."

"Don't forget the root of all this," Anna said. "He's here to help you."

"We should go," Matt said, pushing himself up off the chair. He asked Anna, "I'm assuming you don't need the mirror?"

"No," she said firmly.

"I'll go open the car."

When he'd gone, Mason pulled out his wad of cash, counting out four hundred dollars and handing it to Anna. He felt a twinge of guilt that he was paying her for the séance but not Matt—he hadn't asked for money. Still, he'd pay him for interviewing Etor.

"Thank you," Anna said, and the money quickly disappeared into her bra.

When Matt returned, Mason helped him maneuver the mirror out to the SUV, and Anna bade them good night.

Despite the scant late-night traffic, Matt hunched over the wheel, focusing intently on the streets, a major shift from his usual comfort behind the wheel.

"That was very weird," he said, not looking away from the road. "I'm a little shaken."

"Me too," Mason said.

"You have no control over him, and he looks just like you. If he goes and robs a fucking liquor store, the video will show that it was you."

"I know," Mason said. "Still, I don't think he will. We're still connected somehow."

Matt grunted, and they rode in silence. Mason hardly noticed the dark city rolling by.

Matt parked on the street near Mason's front door and switched off the ignition. "What do we do with the mirror?"

"Do you want it for your apartment?" Mason asked hopefully.

"No fucking way. I'd get nightmares."

"Can you donate it to the thrift store again?"

"I guess," Matt said, looking back at it

dubiously. He grabbed his keys and climbed out, gently closing the door.

"Are you coming in?" Mason asked quietly, confused.

"I'm staying over. My girlfriend lives here, and you and I are working in the morning, remember?"

"Oh—duh. Of course. Come on in."

"Did your doppelgänger get half your brain?" Matt asked as they walked toward the door.

Mason chuckled. "I hope not. It's been a long night."

Matt let himself into Peggy's room, and Mason washed up and then climbed into bed with Ned, who was already sound asleep.

Later he dreamed about a wildfire, burning up a hillside at night, flames leaping and swirling in the darkness. He could feel the heat on his skin. It was too early for fire season, he thought irritably. That was after the summer, before the winter rains. In the distance he noticed a figure, indistinct at first, but soon he saw that it was his doppelgänger, surrounded by flames, their bright orange reflection flickering in his eyes. He wasn't affected by the heat at all, raising his fists to the sky and shouting, exultant—a guttural scream of triumph.

Six

Mason awoke to Ned shaking his shoulder. He rolled over, shielding his eyes from the bright light from the windows.

"Why are you torturing me so early in the morning?" he demanded, slurring the words, his tongue thick and dry.

"I wouldn't wake you unless it was an emergency," Ned said. "We're having pancakes."

"That's worth getting up for. I'll be right out."

When he got there, Ned had just set a platter on the dining table. He sat with Matt and Peggy, and after Ned brought him a coffee, the four of them dug in. Matt seemed to have recovered from his post-séance state of shock, and based on Ned's untroubled mood, no one had told him about the events of last night.

Peggy was already dressed for work, and as soon as she'd eaten, she headed out the front door. Mason helped clean up, then pulled on his backpack, remembering to grab more cash from his desk drawer. He kissed Ned good-bye, and he and Matt went out to the street.

"You look like you're dressed for school," Mason said. Matt was wearing jeans but also sported a collared shirt and a knit necktie.

"I figured you'd present me as a consultant," he said, unlocking his car and climbing in. "I wanted to look the part."

"I didn't tell anyone at Clementine Manor that I was bringing you. That way Etor won't have time to prepare for it."

"Have you heard from your friend from the mirror?" Matt asked, starting the car.

"Not yet. Thanks for not telling Ned about it."

"Thank Peggy. I told her what happened at Anna's—I figured you'd already discussed it in front of her, so it wasn't a secret. But she knew Ned wouldn't have heard about it. She said that was for you to work out with him."

Once they were on the road, Mason summarized Etor's story for Matt, describing what he'd said about Grapalia, his passport, and the point where things had changed for him. It had to be the day he'd arrived, somewhere between the airport, where immigration had recognized his passport, and the currency-exchange bank, where they hadn't.

"What else does he say has changed?" Matt asked, nosing onto the freeway and easing into the slow-moving traffic.

"He thinks Germany is called Austria, and Ireland has a different name. Also New Zealand moved to a different place on the map."

"I can remember all that," he said. "I'll throw it back at him, to see if he contradicts himself."

Even with morning traffic, the drive into the hills was a lot quicker than Mason's train ride and arduous bicycle climb, and they were soon at the gate to Clementine Manor. Matt reached out his window to press the intercom button and gave Rosalía Mason's name.

"Park in front of the leftmost garage door," Rosalía's tinny voice instructed, and they waited as the gate rolled open.

Matt parked where he'd been told, and they climbed out and walked toward the house. When they were halfway across the courtyard, the gravel crunching under their shoes, Eddy stepped out the front door, dressed in his black driver's uniform.

"Hello," Mason said as they passed, and even though Eddy had looked at both of them, he didn't respond.

A few moments later, however, he heard Eddy say, *"Soo-wee."*

"What's his damage?" Matt asked, glancing back.

"I guess I got under his skin the other day. He

actually threatened to break my nose."

"He thinks you're a cop."

"Is that what that meant?" Mason asked, incredulous. "He knows damn well I'm not."

"It's a college football thing. It's how you summon the pigs in the barnyard in the South."

Lowering his voice, Mason said, "I can see why he'd be resentful about cops. He's been arrested a lot."

Rosalía greeted them as they stepped into the foyer, and Mason introduced Matt.

"He'll be talking to Etor today," he explained. And to Matt, "Rosalía runs this place."

"Well, it seems we're in very good hands," Matt said, eyeing her.

Rosalía blushed at that, flashing him the briefest smile, practically batting her eyelashes at him. Was it Matt specifically, or some straight-guy faculty that went over Mason's head? Matt had won her over in milliseconds, while with Mason she was barely civil, even though they'd met repeatedly.

Turning to Mason, she said, "Margaret can't see anyone today."

"Of course she can't," Mason said flatly. "We're here to talk to Etor."

"He should be in his rooms," she said. "Go on up."

Mason led the way up the stairs, rapping sharply on Etor's door. It took him a moment to open it, but once he did, Mason worked quickly.

"This is Matt," he explained. "He's going to

conduct the interview we talked about."

Etor looked annoyed. "I'm not sure I should have agreed to that. I think I'd rather just get on with my new life in this strange place."

"But you did agree to it," Mason insisted. "Henry's counting on it. You're an open book, remember?"

Reluctantly Etor stepped aside, and Mason went in, dropping onto one end of the sofa. Matt followed him, sitting at the other end. Etor joined them but didn't sit down.

"I might take a moment to smoke," he said, and picked up the packet of Gitanes from the coffee table.

"No time for that," Matt said, gesturing to the easy chair.

Etor hesitated but sat, tossing the cigarettes back on the table. He was starting to look a little worried, Mason thought.

"Just a few questions," Matt said, leaning forward.

"As you wish."

"Where did you arrive in the United States?"

"I flew into your local international airport."

"There are a few of them around. You mean LAX?"

"Correct."

"When did you arrive at LAX?"

"Thursday."

Mason was impressed. Matt lobbed his questions quickly, his tone calm but firm, and watched Etor intently.

"Where was the flight from?"

"Madrid. It was a nonstop."

"What was the flight number?"

"I can check."

"Please do."

He scowled but rose from the chair and stepped into the bedroom, reemerging a moment later with a laptop. Mason stood and walked around behind the sofa. He didn't need to be here for the whole interview, but he wanted to get a sense of how it was done.

Etor sat down again, pulling open his computer, and even though Mason couldn't see the keyboard, from his vantage point he could tell what Etor was typing—four rapid jabs at the top row of keys. It was the password to unlock the device, Mason realized, and he tried to figure out what it was. There were four numbers, definitely ending with 2 and then 1, but the first two were less obvious. It had to be either 8-9 or 9-0, he decided. That was enough to break into the computer. He repeated the numbers in his head—8921, 9021.

"Four three four," Etor announced, looking up.

Mason mentally scrambled to retain his own numbers.

"Flight 434," Matt said. "When you arrived, the immigration officer didn't think your passport was unusual?"

"He said 'We don't see many people from Grapalia,' but he recognized Grapalia."

"How do you know that?"

"Because he didn't think it was strange," Etor said, irritated.

"Can I see your passport?"

Etor pressed his lips together and closed his laptop, wordlessly rising again and stepping into the bedroom.

"I'm going to leave you to it," Mason said quietly, briefly resting his hand on Matt's shoulder.

"Good idea," Matt said, turning to look up at him. He added quietly, "It'll work better one-on-one."

Mason left the door ajar and stood in the hall, pulling his notepad out of his backpack and scribbling down the numbers Etor had typed. Once he'd slung his bag back on his shoulders again, he looked up and down the hallway. He knew which door was Deborah's, now firmly closed, but there were many others. A psychic colleague had once taught him a direction-finding technique, and he tried it now, closing his eyes, clearing his mind, and thinking about Margaret. He didn't have a mental image of her, as he'd never seen a photo, so he focused on her name, stretching his mind outward, feeling for insights at the edges of his awareness.

He stood there for some time, tuning out the patter of Matt's questions, but there were no directions forthcoming from beyond the veil—he couldn't find her. He sighed, annoyed, and opened his eyes. There were other ways. Logically, Margaret would have the grandest quarters in the house, having lived here the longest, and that would likely be in one of the corners. Not at the front with a view of the garage, he thought. Much more likely that it would overlook the lush greenery at the back.

Thinking about which way the garden was, he walked farther down the hall, past Deborah's door on the left, to the end, where there was a lone door on the right. That was definitely the direction of the garden, but was this the gateway to the matriarch? He twisted the knob, pushed the door open as quietly as he could, and stepped inside.

Configured differently than the suites where Etor and Deborah slept, this room, at least, looked lived in, even though no one was here now, a bedroom rather than a hotel room. The dark wainscoting matched the style of the foyer, and oil paintings—still lifes, landscapes—hung above the cluttered writing desk, the sprawling vanity, the bed. Windows ran along two sides, looking out on the manicured garden straight back, and on the side, the eucalyptus trees he'd seen from Henry's office, shaggy and wild.

Mason took a few steps toward the windows before he saw her. Sitting in a wing chair, facing the windows, a blanket covering her lap even though the day was warm, she glared at him, her blue eyes sharp beneath her curls of gray hair.

"The matriarch," he said.

"Who are you?" she demanded. Not waiting for an answer, she said, "Get out."

"You sent for me. I'm a friend of Anna's. I've been anxious to talk to you."

"Come over here, where I can see you," she barked, but her eyes betrayed less certainty, her fingers twisting nervously at the arm of the chair.

Mason stepped closer, dropping to one knee a few feet from her chair so that she could see his face.

"That wasn't so difficult, was it?" he said, forcing a smile.

"I'm not accustomed to entertaining strangers in my room," she said, studying him, her fingers still working absently, twisting something black, maybe a piece of string or a bit of cloth.

"In a way I'm not really a stranger. I'm friends with Anna, and I know Henry, and Deborah, even Rosalía."

"Those people are my whole world, since I'm shut up in this house." She looked to the window, her initial alarm replaced with something else, something far away.

"Along with Etor."

"The man from another world," she said, raising her eyebrows, still looking at the garden.

"Does he remember people that you knew? Your relations?"

"He remembers a lot about that side of the family. I married in, so I only knew Cyrus as an old man. Cyrus was the patriarch, the Whitby who made the family fortune. I never met any of Etor's people, the Spanish branch."

"But you believe he's related to you."

"Do you know why Cyrus called this house Clementine Manor?"

"I have no idea." Mason looked around for a chair, wishing she'd invite him to sit, but there weren't any nearby. He dropped his other knee and sat on his feet.

"During prohibition he ran a gambling ship called *The Clementine,* anchored offshore where the police couldn't touch him. People would cruise out there to gamble and drink."

"I read about how Cyrus got his start."

"*The Clementine* is where the money came from, so that's what he called this house."

"Your family has an interesting history."

"The Spanish relatives made their money in similarly devious ways, but they lost it. Manuel—Etor—is the only one left."

"Can I see his letters?" Mason asked.

Margaret looked at him, startled, as if she'd forgotten he was there. "On the secretary," she said, nodding to the little desk. "They're tied with a brown string."

Pushing himself up, he crossed the room to the desk and found the packet.

"Do you mind if I sit here for a minute and look at these?" he called to her.

"Of course not," she snapped.

Untying them, he admired their simple elegance. Letter writing was a craft nearly consigned to history. The envelopes were edged in red and blue and labeled AIR MAIL, the writing paper so thin it was translucent. Thumbing through the stack, he saw that most bore the same Spanish postage stamp and were postmarked twenty-five years ago—except two, with a different stamp and dated earlier this year. All of them were in the same cramped handwriting, signed "Manuel."

He scanned the contents of the oldest one. The tone was breezy and the subject matter not especially personal. The next letter was more gossipy. He realized he was only seeing half of the conversation, with Margaret's replies missing.

The subsequent missive mentioned in passing that Manuel was volunteering at a church. Mason clicked on the lamp above the desk and pulled out his phone, firing up the camera and making sure the flash was off. He photographed several of the pages, capturing Manuel's signature, and the comment about his volunteer work.

Scanning the next letter, a line jumped out at him: "David and I have moved to a smaller home."

"Margaret," he called, turning toward her, "who's David?"

"Manuel's companion. He was an American."

"By 'companion' do you mean a servant, or a husband?"

"His romantic partner. He often wrote about David."

"But you never met either of them."

"That was the point of this trip. We hadn't corresponded in many years, and Manuel wrote to say that David had died. Manuel was going to travel, visiting us here, reconnecting with the only family he had left."

If they'd moved, the return address should have changed. He riffled through the envelopes, and sure enough, there were two, in the same town. The two envelopes postmarked this year bore the second address. He pulled out one of the newer letters. It was in the same hand but shakier, the work of an elderly man. Explaining David's death, he had written "I am rent with sorrow at losing the love of my life." It was poignant, and even though he was a complete stranger, Mason felt sorry for him. The other recent letter, written a month later, proposed Manuel's visit to Los Angeles.

"I saw your reply to this last one," he said to Margaret. "Have you seen it?"

"Etor says there were several letters from me, but he just brought the one inviting him here."

"But you recognized it."

"I didn't write it, but it's in my handwriting. I'd never heard the name Etor before he arrived on our doorstep." She sighed. "I know I don't have to explain it to you and Anna, but there are mysterious forces at work in the world. Things unseen, things impossible to understand. My cousin stumbles through from a parallel world, and he's a completely new person. I can see a tiny corner of it all from right here—the intricacy of the branches and leaves, multitudinous, twisted, random. The way the bark peels off the eucalyptus trees. It's all so complicated. The unseen world must be equally complicated, don't you think?"

"Presumably," Mason said, and then, trying to

draw her back, "The letter that Etor has—was it similar in content to a letter you did write? A letter to Manuel?"

"Very similar, and approximately the same date."

"Do you keep copies of your outgoing correspondence?"

"Unfortunately not. I suppose I should. I always thought it was a little pretentious, the idea that future generations would care about what I had to say."

Photographing the envelope and pages from the last letter, he slipped his phone back into his pants and retied the bundle.

"Have you spent much time with Etor?" he asked, crossing the room to her chair and sitting cross-legged on the floor.

"We've spoken," she said, looking away, the black fabric twisting rhythmically in her hand.

"Does he know things that only your family would know?"

"You're asking if I have any inkling that he might be lying. I don't know how to answer that. I've hardly seen him."

Why would she lie about that? Mason wondered. Rosalía had said they spent lots of time together.

"Still, you believe he's your cousin."

"He is." For the first time, she broke into a smile. "The Spring Affair will be our opportunity to introduce Etor to the inner circle. Perhaps some of my relations will see the family resemblance."

"What's the Spring Affair?"

"The Whitby Spring Affair. Our annual garden party. Right down there."

Mason stood up and followed her gaze out the window. There was certainly enough open space for a party among the flowers and shrubbery, under the oaks and cedars.

"So what have you turned up in your investigation, Mr. Braithwaite? You've been at it for several days now."

He turned to her, surprised at the sudden lucidity. Her eyes were on him, watery but sharp, the only hint of anything amiss the relentless finger work.

"Well, his money is real, so that didn't come from another dimension. I brought a professional interviewer with me today. He's speaking with Etor right now to obtain further information."

"I know Henry is handling your contract, but I'm beginning to think your investigations are unnecessary. Etor is a gentleman, and it's becoming increasingly hard to disbelieve him."

"You just said you've hardly seen him."

She looked up at him, surprised, and then scowled. "I know human nature, and he's a good man. Perhaps you should wrap up your prying."

"That word," Mason said, crossing his arms and leaning back on the window frame. "*Prying.* It makes it sound like I'm doing something illicit. I'm doing legitimate research, and my gut feeling is that there's more to do." He watched her for a moment, her fingers dancing with the scrap of cloth, completely unaware she was doing it. "I also have the feeling that you're not telling me everything."

"You can be very rude," she said, taken aback.

"I'm just doing my job."

She waved her hand dismissively. "That's between you and my son. Henry's a good boy, but he's got a suspicious mind."

"What was he like as a teenager?"

"Mr. Braithwaite, I'm quite tired. Could you please go?"

"By all means," he said, unfolding his arms and standing erect. "Now that we've met, will you let me speak with you next time I'm here?"

"Certainly," she said, but he knew that was likely an empty promise.

He said good-bye and headed for the door. Walking back down the hallway, he could hear Matt still hammering away at Etor, so he walked past the stairs into the other wing of the house. There was another staircase here that led to the ground floor, this one utilitarian, lacking the grandeur of the front stairs, and he followed it down into a service hallway that ended at the kitchen. There was no sign of Rosalía, the room quiet but for the hum of the refrigerator.

Walking the length of the space, he pushed through the garden doors and outside, breathing in the rarified air, humid and scented by cedar. The garden was a lovely, lush space, and he walked its perimeter, admiring the variety of flora and getting a sense of its scale, then wandered over to a bench, setting his backpack beside him. They must be dumping a lot of water out here to keep everything so green.

Pulling out his notepad, he flipped to a clean page and wrote "Margaret Whitby" across the top. He wondered if she was watching now him from her window upstairs, but decided not to look up. He added "matriarch" under her name, and then jotted down some notes:

> nervous; fidgety; distracted—but lucid
> believes Etor's story
> lied for no discernible reason

He put the pad away and then went inside, through the main doors into the hall. From Henry's office he heard a loud guffaw, and then Matt's voice. He went over and stuck his head in.

"Mason," Henry called to him. "Join us."

Henry was in one of the wing chairs, wearing a golf shirt and trousers, leaning toward Matt and grinning like a teenager. How was Matt able to instantly charm everyone he met?

"You brought in the big guns," Henry said.

"I'm lucky to have help," Mason said, and to Matt, "Did you brief Henry about your interview?"

"No—I was just asking Henry some questions," Matt said, his eyes furtively darting toward the door.

It struck him then—Matt wasn't briefing Henry, he was interviewing him too.

"Cool. Listen, I need to spend a few minutes on my notes," Mason said. "I'll be in the garden."

He went back outside and found another bench with a different view. It was clever of Matt to question Henry. He'd get a fuller picture of everything that was going on. Mason had to laugh—Henry didn't even know he was being interrogated.

Content amid the foliage, he spent a few minutes regrouping, clearing his head, letting the calm inherent in the greenery seep in. A sudden thought struck him: if Margaret had invited Manuel to visit, why hadn't he shown up? Were they expected to assume that because Etor had dropped into this world, Manuel had been thrust into his? One man traversing parallel worlds was a stretch, but the phenomenon happening twice in such a neat exchange was too much.

Matt would probably be a few more minutes, he reasoned, and stood up, pulling on his backpack, then entered the house through the door to kitchen and the back stairs. Taking them two at a time, he went back to Margaret's door, glancing back down the hallway to make sure he wasn't being observed. Knocking sharply, he didn't wait for an answer, but stepped inside. She was still in her chair by the window, and looked up at him as he approached.

"One has the right to expect a certain level of privacy in one's own home," she said, not concealing her annoyance.

"I won't be long," he said. "I just had one other question. You wrote letters to Manuel, but did you ever talk to him on the phone?"

"I guess we're both old-fashioned. I only corresponded with him by mail."

"So you only have his mailing address—but no phone number, no email address?"

"Nothing of the kind."

"Thanks, Margaret. That's all I needed to know. I'll be on my way."

Gently closing her door behind him, he went down the back stairs again and out into the garden, lost in thought. He needed to track down Manuel. If he'd disappeared from his own life, maybe Etor was telling the truth, and there was some kind of cosmic tit-for-tat program.

Matt came out into the garden, interrupting his thoughts. "I think I'm finished," he said.

Mason followed him back into the office. Henry was still in the wing chair, scrolling through something on his phone.

"So what's the Whitby Spring Affair?" Mason asked, sitting next to him.

Henry grinned at Matt and waved for him to sit too. "It's a party we hold every year for old business friends and employees. Family too, of course. There are usually about sixty people."

"Can you invite me?" Mason said, glancing toward the door and lowering his voice. "Etor will be at the party, which will give me the opportunity to go through his stuff."

Henry looked appalled. "Is that really necessary?"

"I think it is. In fact, I think there's some urgency. I finally spoke to Margaret today. She says that she believes him—that he's kin. She also lied about how often she's seeing him."

"Oh, god," Henry said, sinking back in his chair.

"There might be clues among his things that back up his story, or contradict it," Mason said. "Plus I'd like to get into his computer."

Henry's eyebrows shot up. "It's just so … distasteful."

"Henry, it's why you hired me. If you could do it yourself, you would have."

He looked from Mason to Matt, considering it. "You could do that anytime," he said finally. "Why does it have to be during the party?"

"Does Etor ever go anywhere?"

"Good point."

"Margaret said the party would be his debut, so she'll be introducing him to people. He won't be hanging out in his room."

"She said that?" Henry asked, incredulous. "So he really has wormed his way in."

"That makes it even more pressing that we get to the truth," Mason said.

"I'll put you on the guest list," Henry said, and sighed.

"Thanks," Mason said, rising from his chair and pulling on his backpack.

"I also wanted to ask you what came of looking into Eddy," Henry said.

"Nothing important. At least not yet."

"I know he's had legal troubles," Henry said. "He's in recovery now, though, and he seems to be keeping it together."

"I'm glad he's been honest with you about his past," Mason said.

They said good-bye, leaving Henry in his office, and walked across the courtyard toward Matt's SUV.

Glancing back toward the front door to make sure they were alone, Mason said, "I didn't get it at first that you were interrogating Henry. Did you get enough time with him?"

"Shh," Matt said, shooting him a warning look.

Mason held his tongue as they got in the car, and they rode in silence until they were headed down the long driveway.

"Such specific instructions about where to park," Matt said, braking to wait for the gate to roll open. "You have to think there's a camera trained on that spot."

"I never thought of that," Mason admitted. "So what did you learn from Etor?"

"Can we go sit somewhere? I can't drive and think after all that intensity, and I'm getting hungry."

"Go down into NoHo. I know a great vegan place."

Mason directed him to the café, and Matt pulled into a metered space right out front.

"I fucking love the Valley," Matt said, turning off the engine. "There's always lots of parking."

At the counter they both ordered falafel

sandwiches and some dolmades, and Mason asked for a triple espresso.

"I wasn't able to catch Etor in a single contradiction," Matt said once they were seated. "If he's lying, he's very good. Either his story is true, or he's extremely well rehearsed in it. And it's all pretty straightforward, despite the weirdness."

"What's straightforward about it?"

"The story is linear, one event after the next, and there aren't a lot of people involved except him. That makes it easier to tell the lie consistently—if it is a lie."

Mason pulled out his notepad and wrote down Matt's impressions, setting it aside when the waiter brought their food.

"Did you get any psychic insight beyond that?" he asked.

"In a way," Matt said, picking up his sandwich. "Even though I couldn't find any clear evidence, my gut instinct is that he's lying."

"What about Henry?"

"He was forthcoming about everything I asked him. He's less slick than Etor, which makes him more believable."

Mason nodded, sipping at his espresso.

"Have you considered that Henry might be collaborating with Etor to trick his mother?"

Mason frowned. "Why would you think that? He seems guileless. Besides, he's the one who hired me."

"Not really. His mother hired you." Matt bit

into a dolma, watching him. "Don't take this the wrong way, but you seem to have a crush on him. That's making you blind, so you're not even suspicious of him."

Mason set down his falafel, struggling to contain his surprise. His first reaction was to hotly deny it, but he pushed that aside. "Why do you think I have a crush on him?"

"Maybe it's subconscious," Matt said, gesturing vaguely, "but it's as plain as the drool on your chin."

Mason snorted. "I'm committed to someone else."

"That doesn't switch off your libido, or your retinas. Anyway, I'm just saying you should consider the possibility. Not everything he says is true. I didn't catch him contradicting himself, but he's hiding something. I can feel it."

"I'm pretty sure he's closeted."

Matt looked surprised. "OK, yeah—that might be it. Come to think of it, he was a bit flirty. Even so, you should make sure there's not more to it."

Mason finished his sandwich, and pulled his wad of cash out of his pants, peeling off three hundreds and handing them to Matt.

"Thanks, man," he said, and quickly pocketed them.

Back in the car, Matt navigated to the freeway, the afternoon traffic already crawling. They rode in silence for a while, Mason worn out from the work and sluggish after eating. He couldn't believe Matt thought he was into Henry. Was it possible it was true? Beyond that, was he so transparent? He was going to have to take a critical look at Henry too.

His phone rang, interrupting his thoughts. "Hey, Peggy," he answered. "I'm with your boyfriend."

"Put me on speaker," she said.

"Hi, babe," Matt said, grinning but keeping his eyes on the stop-and-go traffic.

"Where are you?" she asked, the tiny speaker distorting her voice.

"Driving back to your pad."

"Me too. I'm on my way home from work."

"You left early?" Matt said. "You sound stressed out."

Mason glanced at him; he hadn't detected that.

"More like freaked out," she said. "So I'm downtown today, getting coffee, and who do I see standing in the line in front of me? Mason."

"I wasn't downtown today," he said.

"I know that," she said emphatically. "This person is the same height as you, the same build, the same hair color. But I knew it wasn't you, because you're wearing a green track suit, and a bunch of blingy gold chains around your neck, and you ordered a soy latte. You'd never do that. But when you turned around, I saw your face, and it's you. I asked, 'Mason?' and you were kind of rude." She mimicked Mason's voice. "'You got the wrong guy, pregnant lady. The name is Sam.'"

"Holy fucking balls," Matt said.

"He's got his own name?" Mason asked. He could feel his heart pounding.

"Apparently," Peggy said. "I knew it was your doppelgänger from the mirror because he knew me. I wasn't in costume, but he knew about Peggy Pregnant."

"What did you say he was wearing?"

"A green track suit—bright green polyester. It was weird."

"And you said jewelry?"

"Like, ten gold chains and a medallion the size of your fist. Sunglasses pushed up on his head, with red mirrored lenses, and his hair was all slicked back. He looked so much like you, but he's so not you."

"What else did he say?" Mason asked.

"Nothing—he walked away. Listen, I'm just parking, so I'm going to hang up. I'll see you when you get here."

"We won't be long," Matt said.

"What the hell is he up to?" Mason asked once he'd ended the call. He could feel that his face was flushed, reacting to the news.

"You should check your credit card," Matt said, glancing over at him.

"Damn it," he said, dismayed at the thought. He peered at his phone again, connecting to his bank and scrolling through the transactions. "This morning he spent four hundred at a cell phone store."

"He told you he was going to do that."

"Right ... then a few bucks at a coffee place, two hundred at a sporting goods store, fifty at a thrift store, coffee, coffee ..."

Matt snorted. "He shares your love of the java."

"A *pupusería,* more coffee … then thirty bucks at an Ethiopian restaurant. Why would he be eating Ethiopian food?"

"Why does anyone?"

Mason signed out of his bank and pocketed his phone. "I guess it doesn't seem that crazy. He hasn't bought anything at a knife store. And he hasn't charged any lodging—that's interesting."

"So far, at least," Matt said.

Seven

Matt turned onto Mason's street and parked behind Peggy's car.

"Are you coming in?" Mason asked him.

"I have a thing downtown, but I'll say hi to Peggy."

Twisting his key in the lock, Mason pushed open the front door, then stopped short. His double, Sam, was sitting on the sofa, talking to Ned, who was in an armchair, fingers interlaced behind his head, knees spread apart. Mason knew him well enough to recognize that body language: he was preening. Sam must have been stroking his ego.

It was shocking to see Sam's transformation.

Last night he'd been a perfect copy of Mason, but now he was someone else, and dressed differently again from when Peggy had seen him downtown. From the waist up he looked like an old photo of the scientists in the Apollo mission control room—white shirt and skinny black tie, hair slicked back. But the pants—they were bright red. And weird pointy gray shoes. Were they leather?

"What the hell?" Mason demanded.

Ned turned toward him, a happy grin on his face. "You never told me you had a cousin."

"Yeah, Mason," Sam said. "What the hell?"

"Uh … my family isn't as close as yours," Mason said, talking to Ned but unable to take his eyes off Sam.

"Where's Peggy?" Matt asked, sounding worried.

"Changing out of her work drag," Ned said casually.

"What's going on?" Mason asked, trying to keep his voice even. Sam was leaning toward Ned, and that grin on his face—it all looked way too intimate.

"I'm learning that Sam is a pistol," Ned said.

"He'd better behave himself," Mason said sharply.

"What are you two gawking at?" Ned asked. "Come in and sit down."

They did, Mason on the other wing of the sofa, and Matt between him and Sam, his arms folded.

"Get yourselves a drink, if you want," Ned said. "I'm on tonic water, but Sam's on bourbon."

"You're drinking?" Mason asked Sam, incredulous. "It's not even dark out."

"My rule used to be five o'clock," Ned said.

Mason raised his eyebrows. "And you wound up in AA."

Ned looked puzzled. "I'm sure Sam can take care of himself."

Sam picked up his tumbler from the coffee table and swirled its contents, looking at Mason. "You should have one. Ned opened the good stuff for me," he said, and shot him an exaggerated wink.

Mason recoiled physically at the louche gesture. Was this how he looked to other people?

Peggy appeared from the hallway, free of her workaday black and gray, in a short skirt and a colorful blouse.

"Hey, sweetie," she said, eyeing Matt. "Have you met cousin Sam?"

She was going along with Sam's story, Mason realized. He should probably be grateful that she hadn't told Ned what really happened.

"We met once before," Sam said quickly. "How are you doing?"

"Fine, 'Sam,'" Matt said, looking at him askance.

Ned's eyes narrowed, and he looked at Matt curiously.

Matt avoided his gaze. "I actually have to go. I just wanted to say hello."

"You're going to miss this?" Peggy said.

He rose to embrace her, looking back at Sam, and she walked him to the door. "Keep in touch, Mason," Matt said pointedly, and kissed Peggy good-bye before he left.

"You know, you two look a lot alike," Ned said.

Sam scoffed. "I suppose there are some similarities, but they're completely superficial."

Peggy sat on the sofa where Matt had been and eyed Sam.

"Sure," Ned said. "Your hair is darker."

"That's from whatever jive-ass product he's put in it," Mason said.

"Still, it's uncanny," Ned said, reaching into his pocket. "Can I photograph you two together?"

"No," Mason and Sam said simultaneously, both folding their arms.

"Oh … kay," Ned said, sliding his phone back in his pants.

Sam picked up his tumbler and slurped at the bourbon, eyeing Mason. "Stare much?" he asked.

Peggy laughed, covering her mouth with her hand.

"Are you wearing eyeliner?" Mason demanded.

"It really makes my eyes pop. You should try it."

"The side effects would far outweigh the benefits in Mason's case," Ned said.

Sam frowned. "What does that mean?"

"He means I'd smudge it," Mason said. "I'd get it all over my face, and then all over my shirt. I'd look like a printer cartridge exploded in my hands."

Sam looked at Ned, gesturing with his chin.

"Lucky for you, you don't even need it."

Peggy coughed, covering her mouth again, probably trying to suppress a snicker, Mason thought with some annoyance.

"You have such lovely thick eyelashes," Sam continued.

"Stop flirting with him," Mason said emphatically.

Sam leaned back, draping an arm on the back of the sofa. "I just thought, you know, there's a big empty bedroom down the hall."

Ned's eyebrows shot up.

"Maybe we could mess around," Sam said, as if the implication wasn't already clear.

"That's not going to happen," Mason snapped.

Peggy sat forward. "I don't think I need to hear about this."

Sam guffawed, his head rolling back. "I'm just messing with them, Peggy—don't go."

She hesitated, but sank back onto the sofa.

"Seriously, though. Now that the four of us are here, I can tell you why I've come." He looked at each of them in turn, smirking vaguely, clearly enjoying the attention as they watched him expectantly.

"Well?" Mason demanded, throwing his hands up.

"I can run interference for you at the party," Sam said.

Ned frowned. "What party?"

"The family I'm working for is having a garden

party," Mason said. And to Sam, "What do you mean by 'interference'?"

"You want to ransack Etor's room," Sam said, "but he's wary of you, so he'll be watching you closely. I'll be you at the party to distract him while you go do it."

"'Ransack'?" Ned said dubiously.

"That's actually a freaking great idea," Mason said, relieved that there was finally a point, finally a reason for Sam being here.

"I get to wear the suit," Sam said.

"No way. It's the only decent thing I own."

"You won't even be partying."

"Neither will you," Mason said. "Come on, man. I have such trouble with clothes, and you don't seem to. Although I'm not sure about those shoes."

"These are vintage eighties rat-stabbers," Sam said, extending his foot. "They're very recherché."

"Such a graphic name," Peggy said. "Vivid and yet cruel."

Sam sighed. "Fine—you can wear the suit. Maybe Ned will take me shopping." He winked at Ned, clicking his tongue.

"What kind of party is it?" Ned asked. "Can I go?"

"It's for their relatives and business associates," Mason said. "I can't show up with an entourage."

"Is it big enough that it'll be catered?" Ned asked.

"I'm not sure. Henry said it would be about sixty people."

"It'll definitely be catered. Tell Henry to put me on the waitstaff. I can help out by keeping an eye on things."

"You just want to see these two in action," Peggy said.

"Absolutely," Ned said.

"It would be great to have you there, actually," Mason said. "You could both help keep Etor out of his room."

"At least I look the part," Ned said. "Anywhere west of La Cienega, Anglos assume I'm a waiter or a valet."

"With that amazing haircut?" Sam said. "They must be blind."

Ned grinned, pleased by the compliment.

"You might even be too polished to be a waiter," Peggy said.

"That's actually a good thing," Mason said. "You have no problem mixing with one-percenters. I've seen you do it in your work."

"It's true—they don't make me uncomfortable."

"Let's do it," Mason said, slapping the sofa cushion. "I'll ask Henry if we can put you on the waitstaff."

"Do you know if they have entertainment planned for the party?" Peggy said.

"I have no idea."

"I want in on this too. Tell Henry he needs a vocalist."

Mason smiled. "Peggy Pregnant?"

"I'd have to leave her at home. She's a woman

of the people. For an upscale garden party, I'd bring out the debutante and do some lounge music. I could cobble together a band."

"That's the spirit," Sam said.

"I'll ask Henry," Mason said. "They might already have something lined up, but I'll try to make it work."

"It'd be hilarious," Sam said. "Like we took over the party."

Mason looked at him for a minute. "Have we thought this through? If there are two of us floating around, Etor could catch on."

"You have to show up at different times," Ned said. "Wear the same outfit, and never be in the room together, so you seem like one person."

Sam shook his head impatiently. "Too complicated. You have to go in disguise. Change your hair color, at the very least. There'll only be one Mason to worry about, and that'll be me."

"Why not you in disguise?" Mason said.

"You're the one who'll be prowling around, dummy. I'll be playing you at the party to reassure Etor. Unless you want me to toss his room."

"No—I'll conduct the search," Mason said. "I know what to look for."

Peggy looked at Mason. "How are you going to disguise yourself? It'll have to be realistic."

"We know people who do drag," Ned said. "Billy. We'll get him to help."

"He'll make me look like Mae West," Mason said dubiously.

"He's a skilled artist. I'm sure he can use a light touch."

"Well, he always looks like Mae West." Billy was Filipino, and he had the cheekbones and the performance chops to transform himself convincingly into the long-dead diva.

Sam stood up and straightened his tie. "I have to go."

"Where?" Mason asked.

"I've got stuff to do," Sam said, glaring at him.

"What stuff?" Mason demanded.

"What's it to you?" Ned said, rising from his chair. "You two sound like you need a CoDA meeting."

"At least give me your number," Mason said, standing up as well.

"Why, so you can bug me? I don't think so," Sam said, and strode to the door.

The three of them stood in silence for a moment after he'd gone.

"Well, that was weird," Peggy said.

"He's family," Ned said simply. "Weird, but welcome. And how cool is it that he can collaborate with you on your case?"

"Hopefully you guys too," Mason said. "That would be great."

"I need to chill before dinner," Peggy said. She looked tired, Mason realized. "Nedly, do you need help?"

"Nope. I'm going to do a mushroom risotto. I'll let you know when it's ready."

Mason went into the office and opened his computer, but before he had time to gather his thoughts, Peggy came in and quietly closed the door.

"Cousin Sam?" she said, arching her eyebrows.

"I didn't come up with that. I was as surprised as you were."

"I can't believe you created him," she said intently.

"He created himself. I just set him loose."

"He's nothing like you."

"I know. But so far, at least, I think he's behaving. He hasn't spent a ton of my money yet."

"What about fawning over your boyfriend?"

"Yeah, there's that." Mason thought about it. "I guess it was harmless."

"I'm glad you think so," she said, absently pushing a hand through her hair. "Why did I run into him today, in a city of ten million people? Do you think he's following me? It kind of creeps me out."

"Where did you see him?"

"In line for coffee at Union Station."

"I know he's been buying a lot of coffee. You're not usually there, are you?"

Peggy thought about it. "Not very often. I guess I strayed onto his turf, not the other way around."

"That's a relief."

"Still, it was weird that he knew who I was."

"It gets weirder. He knew about the Whitbys' party, even though I just found out about it today."

"You're still connected," she said. "What's weird about that? You've talked about psychic backchannels—communication running through the world unseen."

"That must be the explanation. But he doesn't know everything, like why I wouldn't wear guyliner. Shouldn't he know that stuff too?"

She sighed and gestured helplessly. "Listen, are we OK with lying to Ned about who he is?"

"He lied, not me," he said, shrugging.

"Mason, not telling him the truth means you're lying too," she said, exasperated.

"Let's go with it for now." It made him feel queasy, admitting that he was so blatantly deceiving Ned. He could rationalize it away by saying Ned wouldn't believe it anyway, but deep down he felt guilty, despite the extraordinary circumstances.

"Fine," Peggy said. "I need to lie down."

After she'd gone, he considered making some notes about Sam, but decided against it. He had to think of him as an ally, not a problem to be solved. More pressing was Manuel Whitby. Mason read through the notes he'd made earlier and pulled up the images of Margaret's letters, then looked up the return addresses in Spain that were written on the envelopes. Both were easy enough to locate on a map, in a little town in the south, near Seville, but neither address turned up a connection to Manuel's name. Maybe records were kept differently in other countries, he decided. Europeans had different ideas about what constituted public and private information.

A broader search for Manuel turned up a

twenty-year-old item in a Spanish newspaper, and after a rough translation he was able to figure out that it was a story about Easter Week festivities. Manuel Whitby had been participating as a representative of a church called Pillar Virgin, which was in the same little town as his addresses—it had to be the same guy.

Scanning the original Spanish-language text, he saw that the name of the church was actually Virgen del Pilar. It wasn't obvious to Mason whether it was named after a pillar, as the software suggested, or for a virgin named Pilar, or whether Pilar was one of the many incarnations of the Virgin Mary, but the name of the town, at least, wasn't garbled, and it was easy to find a phone number there for the Virgen del Pilar. Even though the article describing Manuel's involvement dated back decades, maybe someone there would know him.

Ned stuck his head in the door and said, "Ready for the best risotto you've ever eaten?"

"Hell, yes."

Peggy looked a little more relaxed at dinner, Mason thought, and Ned's mushroom risotto perked them all up.

"What kind of music would you do at the Whitbys' party if they hire you?" Mason asked between mouthfuls.

"Jazz standards," she said. "Lots of musicians already know the songs, so you don't have to rehearse a lot."

"I would love to hear you do that stuff," Ned

said. "What about your thing tomorrow—are you all rehearsed for that?"

"As much as I can be. It's not really the kind of thing that can be practiced."

"It sounds mysterious," Mason said.

She grinned at him. "You'll see what I mean tomorrow."

"I have a favor to ask of the lone Spanish speaker in the house," Mason said, turning to Ned. "I need you to make a phone call."

"Very few people around here can't speak English," Ned said, setting down his fork.

"Tell that to your *abuelo*."

Ned chuckled. "He understands everything you say—he just doesn't want to give you the satisfaction of speaking his second language. He thinks you should practice yours."

"It's not a local call," Mason said. "It's to actual Spain. I can pay you for the work."

"You're not going to pay me. I helped you do your taxes, remember? You can't afford me."

After they'd eaten, Mason helped clean up a little, then went into their shared office and sat at his desk. He hunted some more for Manuel, but couldn't find anything else that mentioned him. Eventually Ned came into the office.

"Should we make that phone call?" he asked. "I just checked the time difference. It's 8 a.m. there now."

"Take a look at this," Mason said, and handed him the printout of the article he'd found. "I got a number for this Pilar church. Maybe you could ask if Manuel is still involved, and how I can contact him."

"Why should I say I'm looking for him?" Ned asked. "They'll know I'm Latin American from the way I speak."

"Tell them the truth. His American cousin, Henry Whitby, is trying to track him down."

Ned sat at his desk and made the call, pen and paper at the ready. Mason stood nearby, propped on the edge of his own desk. Ned's Spanish sounded polite, but the only words he recognized were Manuel's name and *Los Ángeles*. Ned scribbled something on his notepad and ended the call.

"Success?" Mason asked hopefully.

"Not exactly. The clerk in the office didn't know Manuel, probably because it was so long ago. He did have the name of a priest who was there at the time, but not his phone number. I can call this other church office to try to track him down."

"Excellent," Mason said.

"Let's hope he's still alive," Ned said, and dialed the number he'd written down, then chatted for a few minutes, writing more on his pad.

"They won't give me the priest's number," Ned said, setting down his phone, "but it sounds like he's alive, and she did say his full name: José Antonio del Monte."

"I wonder if I can find him with that."

"Let's try," Ned said. "Do you want me to help?"

"Sure." Mason crouched behind Ned's desk chair as he found a people-search site for Spain, and soon came up with a list of three men with the same name, each with a different phone number.

"It should be one of these guys," Ned said, and dialed the first one. "No answer. That doesn't sound like a priest, still asleep at this hour."

"Maybe he's at work," Mason said.

"I think he's just lazy," Ned said, and grinned at him, dialing the next number, where he got an answer—and got into a lengthy discussion.

Mason retreated to his desk, listening intently, his excitement growing as the phone conversation continued. He heard Manuel's name mentioned, and "David"—Manuel's partner, Margaret had said. Maybe Ned was on to something. And then "*México*."

"It was the priest," Ned said after he'd hung up.

"I figured," Mason said.

"He totally remembers Manuel, and his friend David."

"His husband," Mason said. "Margaret knew about him."

"I wondered if that was what he meant," Ned said. "A priest wouldn't say 'husband' about two men, god forbid."

"What else did he say?" Mason said impatiently.

"They emigrated."

"To Mexico."

Ned grinned. "Close. New Mexico. He said Manuel's friend was from there."

"His husband," Mason said. "Margaret said that too: David was an American. When did they leave?"

"He said it was a long time ago, probably not long after that newspaper article."

"That makes no sense. It would explain why there's no trace of him in Spain since then, but Margaret was corresponding with him at an address in Spain earlier this year."

"Maybe the priest is talking about a different Manuel," Ned said. "It's a common name."

"But Whitby isn't. Not in Spain. And there are too many other common points: the church, David, David being an American. It's the right guy, I'm sure of it." He laughed and slapped the desktop.

"What's so funny?"

"The whole thing is starting to crack open. I don't have all the answers yet, but I can feel it." It was the first clear hole he'd found in Etor's story, and it felt like a rush. It didn't explain everything, but the letters from Spain might—and that meant he really needed to talk to Manuel.

Ned grinned. "I love seeing you so happy, enjoying your work."

"I'm lucky to have your help with this part," Mason said. "Did the priest know what city in New Mexico?"

"Unfortunately not. But a state is a good start."

"Thanks for all that."

Ned stood and stretched his arms over his head. "Bedtime?"

"I'm going to look for Manuel," Mason said, pulling open his computer. He was making headway, and the question now was evident: if Manuel had left Spain back then, how could Margaret be getting letters from him from Spain this year?

"Why not come to bed, and do that in the morning?" Ned said.

He considered that, looking at the little clock on his computer. It was almost midnight. "Yeah, that's probably wise," he admitted, and followed Ned down the hall.

Before he went to sleep, as he was silencing his phone, Ned rolled toward him, wrapping a sleepy arm around his waist. He was about to set the phone down, but decided to send Henry a quick text.

Are you around tomorrow? I'd like to have a chat.

He plugged in the phone and set it face down on his bedside table, then switched off the light. The phone's screen flicked on again briefly, its glow leaking out around the edges. An incoming text. Why was Henry up so late? He picked it up to check, and grinned at his eager reply.

Sure, Mason, drop by. I'd be happy to see you.

Later, he found himself floating, weightless, in a cramped little space capsule. He was wearing a space suit and a heavy helmet. Despite the encumbrances, he could see the stars outside the porthole, serene and stately as they drifted by, so vivid, almost alive. He thought about trying to take charge of the dream, come to some awareness and manipulate things, but the view was too lovely, so he just sat back and enjoyed it.

Eight

As he was waking up, he knew there was something he had to do, though he wasn't sure what. It was just a vague idea at first, as he lay there, enjoying the warmth of the covers, the May-gray light diffusing in the window, the idea slowly coalescing as he came up into consciousness.

Eventually he remembered: find Manuel.

Peggy was long gone, and Ned was immersed in his work in the office. Mason made a pot of espresso, and another, then pulled on a sweatshirt and took his computer out onto the balcony. It was easier to hunt for Manuel when the records were in English, and knowing what state he was in narrowed the results considerably. Soon he had tracked down a phone number and an address linked to Manuel's name, in the town of Alamogordo, but the recording that answered when he dialed told him the number wasn't in service.

Checking a map, he located Alamogordo, in the southern part of the state, at the foot of a mountain range. Nearby was a vast white expanse—White Sands National Park, it was labeled, and next to it, Holloman Air Force Base, which he knew was notorious for its role in the flying saucer phenomenon. Zooming in on the overhead images, he discovered that the address for Manuel was a bungalow on a suburban street. He went into the office and pulled Ned's attention away from his work.

"Is there a way to find out who owns a specific house?"

"Lots of ways," Ned said, leaning back in his chair and lacing his fingers behind his head. "If it's been sold recently, real estate sites will have all the details. Failing that, the county has tax records."

Mason wrote down the names of several websites Ned recommended, and then went back to the balcony. When he looked up the property he found that someone named David Schaffer had sold the house less than two years ago. That could be Manuel's David, he thought, his excitement growing. But he couldn't find a phone number for David, despite digging through several people-search aggregators.

Alamogordo wasn't that big a city, he reasoned, so there couldn't be too many real estate companies. He found a list of them online and dialed one, then another, finally getting somewhere on the third try.

"My friend David Schaffer recommended the agent who sold his house," Mason said, reciting the address, "but I can't remember the agent's name."

"I think I know who handled that sale," the receptionist said, and a minute later he was talking to her.

"Sure, I remember David," she said. "Are you in the market yourself?"

"I might be," Mason lied. "I'm an acquaintance of Manuel's, so I only saw the house once, but I liked the neighborhood."

"That was so sad about Manny," she said.

"Did he die?" Mason asked. "I hadn't heard that."

"Oh, god, no. I meant him moving into assisted living."

"Right," Mason said, and thinking quickly, added, "I haven't been to the facility. Is it nice, at least?"

"He's in the one by the golf course, right? I haven't been there either," she said. "I'm sure David would have found the best possible environment for him."

"I know he would."

"I guess none of us are getting any younger," she said. "So what kind of square footage are you looking for, Mr.—you know, the front office didn't give me your name."

"Listen," Mason said, "I'm going to have to call you back. There's a police car behind me with the flashers on. I think he wants me to pull over." He disconnected the call before she could protest, grinning to himself. That had been a productive call. It was the right David, and even though he didn't have a phone number, he'd learned where Manuel was.

Looking for nursing homes and care facilities and cross-referencing them with a map, there was only one located beside a golf course in Alamogordo.

"I'm calling for Manuel Whitby," he told the receptionist.

"Oh, yes," she said. There was recognition in her voice—this was the right place.

"Does he have his own phone line?"

"I'm sorry, but I can't redirect your call," she said, her tone becoming guarded.

"But he's there."

"I can't give out patient information. Are you a relative?"

"I'm working for a relative. Why can't I talk to him—is he in a coma or something?"

"I'm sorry I can't help you," she said, and hung up.

He pulled up the website for the facility, scrolling through the list of services, staffers, images of the common areas. It didn't seem to be designed for intensive nursing. The residents were portrayed in the photos as active and functional. That meant Manuel probably wasn't a dementia patient or otherwise cognitively debilitated.

Setting the computer on the table, he sat back

and put his feet on the railing, looking out over their hilly neighborhood, the colors muted in the diffuse light. So Manuel was still present in this version of reality. His guardians weren't going to put him on the phone, but Mason could definitely talk to the guy if he went out there, maybe by posing as a relative. It wouldn't be the first time he'd breached low-level barriers like a reception desk. But was it worth the effort?

Picking up his laptop again, he quickly found that the easiest way was to fly into El Paso and drive to Alamogordo from there. He could probably do it one long day, with a connection in Phoenix and returning to the airport in Burbank. It would be annoying, but it was doable. The flights weren't even that expensive, although that was Henry's concern.

He decided to do it. It was the only way to sort out the discrepancy in Margaret's letters. Maybe someone who worked for Henry would book it for him—he was headed over there anyway.

Riding the metro under the hill, standing with his bicycle and watching the concrete walls flash by, he thought about what Matt had said. How much was he missing by not being objective about Henry? Even today, did he really need to see him? Things always went better in person, he knew, so it wasn't just about an alleged crush. He resolved to try to think clearly about Henry, and not cut him any slack.

At the gate to Clementine Manor he told Rosalía his name, and stashed his bicycle beside the garage. Rosalía wasn't in the foyer, but Henry's office door was open, so he went in, knocking gently on the door frame.

Henry looked up from his desk, then rose, looking at Mason over his glasses. "The psychic detective," he said, and waved to the wing chairs. He was wearing a burgundy cardigan, even though it wasn't cold enough for that.

"How are you?" he said as they sat down.

"I'm curious," Mason said, furrowing his brow and fixing him with a hard look. "Did you ever think about trying to find Manuel?"

Henry looked taken aback. "That's why I hired you."

"Right," Mason said. He knew in that moment he really had no reason to be suspicious of Henry. Matt had been wrong about that. His swagger deflated, he shifted in his chair, speaking more gently. "I may have found him."

"Where?"

"New Mexico. I have to go out there and talk to him. It may expose some flaws in Etor's story."

"Doesn't he have a phone?" Henry asked, frowning.

"He doesn't, actually. Besides, interviews tend to work better face-to-face. I'm thinking I'll go tomorrow, so I'll have Saturday to prep for your party."

"I can't believe he's in New Mexico. He said he was coming from Spain."

"That's a big part of why I want to talk to him, that inconsistency. Airfares to get out there aren't too insane, so I'll tack that on as an expense, unless you have someone who books your travel?"

"It's just a one-day trip, out there and back?" he asked.

"That's the plan. There's a connection in Phoenix, and I'll have to get a car."

"If you're going tomorrow, you can take my plane."

"Oh," Mason said, surprised. "With you?"

Henry smiled. "I wish I had the time. With my staff. I'll have someone work it out with you. Give me a second." He pulled out his phone and swiped at it, then started thumb-typing.

When he looked up, Mason said, "The other thing I wanted to talk to you about is the party. Could you put a couple of my people on the staff for it? I assume you're having it catered, so one of them could pose as a waiter."

"Why do you need people there?"

"To keep an eye on Etor while I search his room. I don't have all the facts yet, but finding Manuel makes it look more like he's playing Margaret."

"That's not good news," Henry said, his face clouding. "She seems quite enamored of him. After his pushback the other day, I began to suspect he's acting the gigolo when they're alone up there. It's sick, in a way, if they're supposed to be cousins."

"Then let's nip it in the bud," Mason said. "And let's do it right—put more eyes on him."

"How many people?" Henry asked, shifting in his chair. "Is it Matt? He was quite charming."

Mason grinned. It was an interesting assessment of someone who had ostensibly been interrogating him. "Not this time. I'd like to put two people on staff, and invite my cousin Sam as a party guest. He looks a lot like me, so Etor won't get suspicious—he'll see that I'm at the party the whole time. I'll be in disguise, so I can act without him noticing, and search his room."

Henry rocked forward. "Such intrigue," he said, his eyes bright. "You're bringing an unprecedented element of skulduggery to the Spring Affair. It's so exciting."

"Hopefully there won't be any excitement at all. Your guests won't know anything is going on. And to keep things simple, let's not tell Margaret or anyone else."

"Right—strictly between us," Henry said. "I'll have to tell the party planner, of course. I'll get her to call you." He looked to his phone again. "Her name is Val. Two waiters?"

"One waiter, and one lounge singer."

Henry's eyebrows shot up. "We don't usually have entertainment."

"She's very low-key, and easy to work with."

"It's a big garden. I'm sure Val will find space for her," Henry said, and went back to typing on his phone. "I'll also tell the security guys. They don't need to know what you're up to, just to let you move around freely."

"Do they work for Val?"

"No, directly for me. There'll be three or four of them. If they question your movements, tell them your name, and they'll stay out of your way."

"Are they armed?"

He shook his head, still working on his phone. "They're plainclothes, except a guy in uniform at the front gate. He's also not going to be armed."

"My people won't be armed either," Mason said. Even the subject of firearms made him queasy. "That way, there won't be any surprises."

"You mean like a shootout?" Henry said, looking up, his eyes wide. "Indeed, let's do all we can to prevent that." He studied Mason for a moment. "You're so butch."

Mason laughed. "I don't hear that very often."

Henry was looking at him intently, his eyes soft, his phone forgotten. Mason knew that look. It was an open door. How easy it would be to stray, to connect with Henry right now. These opportunities were rare, because he didn't seek them out, but here one was. Holding his gaze for one second too long would send him down an irrevocable path, down the far side of the mountain. But he had almost let something similar happen recently, when he'd been on a case and a drag queen had kissed him in a bar. It had hurt Ned, damaged his trust. He wasn't going to do that again.

Mason looked away, then sat forward, rising from the chair. The spell was broken.

"I'll look forward to hearing what you find in

New Mexico," Henry said, standing up and slipping his phone into his pocket, businesslike once again.

"I'll let you know," Mason said, flashing him a grin.

Walking out the front door into the fresh air, he turned his face to the sky, letting the gray light wash away the intensity of the moment. Climbing on his bicycle and navigating down the driveway, he felt lighter, relieved. He'd been wise not to linger.

By the time he got down into NoHo he was craving caffeine, and stopped by the coffee place, where he bought a few vegan cookies. When he glanced at his phone he saw that he had missed three calls. Since there was no band playing today and the place was quiet, he sat at a table in the corner and listened to his messages. One was from Miss Cassie, and the other two were from 310 numbers—the Westside. Probably Henry's people.

The first voice message was from a deferential-sounding guy named Max.

"I run the Whitbys' flight service," he explained. "Let's speak at your earliest convenience."

Next was Val, Henry's caterer. "Call me back anytime," she said, her dialect Northeastern, maybe New York. "If you're in Hollywood you can also stop by my office until four."

Miss Cassie never phoned him, and she hadn't left a message, so he called her back first.

"Mason," she said. "Lovely to hear your voice. Sam is coming to see me tomorrow, and I wanted to move his appointment up an hour. I don't have his number, but I'm thinking you could get word to him."

"Sam? Why is he coming to see you?" he said sharply. A patron at another table looked up at him curiously.

"Surely you've heard the phrase 'patient confidentiality.'"

"Is it about me?" he said, struggling to keep his voice down and avoid attracting more attention.

"As unlikely as it sounds, the world doesn't revolve around you," she said.

He could feel his face heating up, his temples throbbing. Of course it was about him, whether Sam told her that or not. What the hell was he up to?

"Fine. I'll let him know if I see him," he said, and ended the call.

He took a couple of deep breaths and ate a cookie, then dialed the number Max had called from.

"Hello, Mr. Braithwaite," he answered. "How are you?"

"Uh—I'm good," Mason said, caught off guard by the familiarity. "You seem to be on top of things."

"I recognized your number," he explained. "I understand we're going to New Mexico tomorrow. Can I ask what airport, and what time you have to be there?"

"I'm going to Alamogordo. I guess it would be good to get there early, maybe ten?"

"Give me a moment," Max said, and Mason waited, listening to Max clacking on his keyboard. "All right—I'll send a car at six thirty, will that work for you?"

"To pick me up?" Mason asked. "That would be brilliant."

Max asked for Mason's address, then said, "Look for a town car at six thirty."

"I will—thanks," he said, resisting the urge to ask what a town car was. Ned would know. Whatever it was, it would certainly be more comfortable than cycling. He bit into another cookie. Henry was saving him a lot of time and effort. It must be nice to have those kinds of resources.

He decided to drop in on Val the caterer, rather than phoning her. Her office was practically on the way home. Climbing up out of the metro in Hollywood, he was happy to see the sun had burned through the marine layer, and enjoyed its warmth as he cycled the few blocks to the address Val had given him, on a side street in the old industrial part of the neighborhood.

Her office looked more like a retail storefront, he thought as he locked his bike to a parking meter. The sign above the door read PARTY WITH VAL in large purple letters. It made him chuckle. She had to know it implied sex and drug use more than garden parties. Who was this woman?

The door was locked when he pulled on it, so

he looked around for a bell. A faint chime sounded somewhere inside when he pressed it, and soon the lock snapped open for him. The interior looked like a shop, with a long counter, but there was no receptionist.

Val soon appeared in the doorway behind the counter. She was in her fifties and had a mane of wild hair streaked with gray. "You must be Mason," she said, smiling at him as she stepped up to the counter.

"Guilty."

"I knew it was you—Mr. Whitby said you were a tall drink of water."

"Henry said that?" Mason asked, incredulous.

"He also said you were a redhead. Either way, you're hard to miss, brother."

He grinned, acknowledging that. She was so upbeat. Party planning had to be a perfect career for her.

"I don't really have anywhere to sit, so we'll have to work at the counter. Let me get my computer." She went into the back, pushing through the swinging door. Mason caught a glimpse of a tall rack shelving stacked with food containers.

Val set her laptop on the counter and pulled it open. "So," she began, peering at her screen, "Mr. Whitby says you're running a security op, and we're going to put some of your operatives on staff."

"Correct," he said. *Operatives*. That certainly gave it more gravity.

"I just need each person's name and number, and we'll set it up."

Mason pulled out his phone to find the numbers.

"Are they all legal to work?"

"They are," he said, meeting her eye.

"It's not that important, but it simplifies the paperwork."

"The waiter's name is Edgar Vélez," he said. "We call him Ned."

She nodded and worked her keyboard. "Will he actually do any work, or just pretend to be a waiter?"

"I suppose a little of both. I know he's willing to work."

She smiled. "I don't need him to. He's on Mr. Whitby's dime. But I wanted to know if I'll need another waiter."

"Maybe count him as half."

After she'd finished typing he gave her Peggy's details.

"I suppose we'll set up a little stage," Val said. "Does she need to be close to the entrance, or can we put her somewhere else?"

"It won't matter. As long as she can see the guests."

"I assume she'll have backing musicians?"

"She will—I don't have their names, but Peggy will fill you in."

"Is Mr. Whitby paying the band, or are you?"

"I hadn't thought of that. I'd rather he did, if he's willing."

"I'll let you know if he can't," she said, and clacked away at her keyboard. "Mr. Whitby never requests music, but it'll be a nice touch."

"You can work out with her how much you want her to perform, or how much Henry thinks she should perform. For my purposes it doesn't matter. I just need her eyes on the crowd." He felt a twinge of guilt at the lie—he didn't need Peggy to be there at all. But it didn't matter to Val, who seemed content with arranging it.

"Are you handling the guest list as well?" he asked.

"I am."

"Besides me, can we add my cousin Sam?"

"You're already listed," she said, peering at her screen. "What's Sam's last name?"

"Uh … the same as mine," he said.

"Anyone else?" she asked, looking up at him.

"I think that covers it."

"So—the guest list is handled at the front gate, and they won't check IDs unless they think something's fishy. Can I give you my cell number in case you need to get in touch before the event?"

"If it's the number you called me from earlier, I've got it," Mason said.

"That's it." Her expression turned serious. "Just so I know, can I ask if there will be any actions?"

"What do you mean?"

"Are you planning to do a takedown, or arrest someone?"

"Not at this time," he said carefully. "It's all

undercover. Ideally no one will notice anything unusual."

She smiled. "Well, I'll look forward to seeing you there."

"Is there anything vegan on the menu, or should I eat before I get there?"

"Mr. Whitby's daughter, Deborah, is vegan, so some of the food will be, and half of the canapés."

"Sweet," Mason said, and headed out to the street.

Ned's baby, his classic seventies Barracuda, wasn't in the garage when he got home, and the house was quiet. He had the place to himself, so he stretched out on the sofa, and started to drift into sleep in the late-afternoon sun streaming through the French doors.

His bliss was short-lived, as Ned came in the front door, carrying shopping bags, followed closely by Sam, a garment bag slung over his shoulder. Mason sat up, blinking awake.

"Sam shops like a gay guy," Ned announced, depositing the bags on an easy chair.

"Sam is a gay guy," Sam said.

"It's weird that you two have so much in common," Ned said. "Why don't we see you more?"

Before he could answer, Mason said, "What did you buy?"

"The most exquisite tux," Sam said, patting the garment bag, then draping it over the back of the chair. "Midnight blue."

Mason grimaced. "Ouch."

Sam leaned toward him and stage-whispered, as if Ned wouldn't be able to overhear. "It wasn't that expensive. You can wear it when I'm done with it."

"I don't think the Spring Affair is supposed to be black-tie," Mason said.

"Who cares?" Sam said. "I'm going to look amazing."

"You mean Mason's going to look amazing," Ned said, smirking at him.

"Right," Sam said. "But *I'll* know it's me."

"I'm glad you're clear on that," Ned said, bemused. And to Mason, "I talked to Billy. He'll come over on Saturday morning to get you tarted up."

Mason frowned. "The party's not till evening."

"Yes, but it'll take time to, uh"—he searched for the words—"take the edge off."

Sam snorted, giving Mason the once-over. "Maybe you should get him over here to start now."

Ned chuckled and went down the hall.

Once he'd gone, Mason asked, "Why are you seeing my shrink?"

"She's my shrink too, technically. I cried in our very first session."

"You *cried*? Why? I've never cried with her."

"Well, she's very good," he said, gesturing vaguely. "It felt like a safe environment. Anyway, I had some family stuff I wanted to tell her about. Next session, I'll fill her in on your attachment thing."

"You keep out of my attachment thing," Mason hissed.

"It's nothing bad. I just have a slightly different perspective. So why did she tell you I was seeing her?"

"She didn't have your number. She wants you to go in an hour earlier."

Sam threw up his hands. "How difficult was that? You could have just said it without all the drama."

"I don't do drama," Mason snapped. "And why are you so damn flirty with Ned?"

"It's not serious. I'm just having a little fun, and he should too—you never go shopping with him."

"We go to thrift stores all the time."

"That doesn't count."

Mason stared at him. It was true, Ned didn't find thrift stores satisfying the way Mason did.

"Do you remember that dick developer guy with the glass office who threw you out on the street when you were on the Penstock Canyon case? What's his name?"

"Douglas Grankin?"

"That's right," Sam said, nodding.

"Why do you ask?" Mason said. And lowering his voice, "And if you're part of me, why don't you know that?"

"I'm not part of you anymore," he said simply. "We have separate experiences now, and we remember things differently."

"I don't get that. Why does it work that way?"

"Do you really want another exact copy of *you* getting up in your grill?" he demanded. "That's not what you need."

"What *do* I need? A double to work Henry's party? There has to be more to it."

Sam pulled out his phone and glanced at it. "Listen, I have to go. Can you hang up my tux? I don't want it to get wrinkled. And don't try it on, either," he admonished. "I don't want it messed up."

"Where are you sleeping, anyway?" Mason asked.

He put his hands on his hips. "Have you ever heard of Grindr, Gladys? All this"—he made a swooping two-handed flourish over his abdomen, ending by lewdly grabbing his crotch—"is very much in demand."

"I've got the same 'all this,' and I've never felt that way in my life."

Sam shrugged. "It's all about how you work it. You're monogamous—you don't need to bother."

With that, he was gone, and Mason sank back onto the sofa.

"Where's Sam?" Ned asked, walking back into the room.

"He had to go. He asked me to hang up his tux."

"I'll take care of it." He dropped onto the sofa, folding Mason's hand into his own. "It's a great color—you'll love it."

"You seem to love him."

"Sure I do," he said simply. "He's a lot of fun, and he's family."

"So I'm going to Alamogordo, New Mexico, tomorrow. Just for the day."

Ned broke into a broad grin. "Right on. You found Manuel."

"I did," he said, and told Ned about the research he'd done. Talking about it calmed him down after his conversation with Sam.

"It sounds like you've almost figured it out," Ned said finally.

"It feels like I'm close. I'll definitely know more tomorrow."

"I can drive you to the airport. Are you leaving from LAX?"

"Henry's actually sending me on his airplane, or maybe it's his company's airplane. Someone's picking me up."

"Wow," Ned said, raising his eyebrows. "You need to get more clients like Henry, and maybe a case with clues on Maui."

"Funny. You know, I think Henry needs a boy-friend. Who can we set him up with?"

"Can't he find his own dates?"

"I get the feeling his world is pretty conformist. He probably doesn't get the chance to meet guys."

Ned sighed. "Well, what's he like?"

"In his forties, maybe. Kind of an executroid. Salt-and-pepper hair, nice smile, good manners."

"And rich," Ned added pointedly. He looked pensive, absently massaging Mason's hand. "Did you ever meet Bart?"

"Maybe. He's kind of tall?"

"Correct."

"You work with him?"

"Sort of—he's a real estate guy, and wealthy, or at least looks wealthy, so he's no stranger to Henry's world. I know he's been single for a while, so I bet he'd be up for an intro. Do you think Henry's afraid of black people?"

Mason frowned. "Why would you think that?"

"He's old money. You kind of expect old money to be racist."

"Well, I doubt Henry is. His daughter's African American."

"Bart's roots are in Suriname, or maybe it's Guyana."

"Let's assume Henry's not racist," Mason said. "Ask Bart if he's free Saturday evening, and I'll put him on the guest list. We can steer them toward each other at the party."

"You're going to have a lot to do. Are you sure it should be then?"

"If I'm busy, you or Sam can handle the introduction. The rest is up to them. I won't tell Henry it's an intro. But you should tell Bart we're setting them up, and tell him Henry doesn't know that."

Ned groaned. "That's too complicated."

"It'll be fine," Mason said. "What's the worst thing that could happen?"

"Bart will hate me, and dedicate himself to burning down my career. Henry will use his deep pockets to sue us until we're homeless."

"That's not going to happen."

"You're probably right. I'll go talk to him now," Ned said, and rose, stretching his arms behind his back. "I was going to do a quick stir-fry before we go to Peggy's thing. How about string beans and peppers?"

"I'm in," Mason said.

After they'd eaten he put on a dress shirt, and even tucked it in. Ned changed clothes too, and as they were walking out, Mason admired Ned's look, effortlessly sharp and polished.

"Always the hottest guy in the room," Mason said, pulling him close for a kiss.

Ned laughed and said, "Don't muss my hair."

"I can't," Mason said flatly. "It looks great no matter what."

Ned locked the door and followed Mason to the garage. "The Barracuda, or the Crown Vic?" he asked.

"This event represents a new genre for Peggy, and we need to arrive in the correct frame of mind. I think there's only one possible answer."

"The Barracuda," Ned said confidently, and soon he was easing the pristine vehicle out of the garage.

"What's the venue?" Mason asked. "I never asked her."

"It's an actual theater—one of those ninety-nine-seat places on Santa Monica Boulevard."

Once they were in the neighborhood, Ned drove slowly past the front entrance, trolling for a parking spot.

Mason read the name of the show on the marquee. "*Three Sensible Women,*" he said. "Not the most electrifying title."

Ned snorted and turned onto a side street, backing into a space.

The theater was already half full, and Mason didn't recognize any of the faces in the crowd from Peggy Pregnant's folk music performances.

"Let's sit down front," Ned said, gesturing to the first row.

Mason sat, and Ned draped his jacket over his seat. "I'm going to the snack bar to chastise them for not having any vegan snack treats. Do you want a coffee?"

"It's too late for caffeine. How do you know they don't have vegan snacks?"

"Just a hunch. We should save a seat for Matt too," he said, and went back to the lobby.

Matt soon wandered in, nodding when he caught sight of Mason, then sat beside him. "Any word from Cousin Sam?" he asked quietly.

"Ned took him shopping today, and he's been to see my shrink."

"Seriously?" Matt stared at him. "You should take him to the mall and get your portrait taken together."

Mason chuckled. "At least I know why he's here. He's going to run interference while I search Etor's room on Saturday."

"Bringing your doppelgänger to life sounds like overkill for that simple problem. It's like buying a new house because a lightbulb burned out at the old one. Are you sure that's all there is to it?"

Mason gestured helplessly. "Maybe there's more, but I'm not seeing it."

"Going to see your shrink sounds like he's moved way beyond helping you with Etor," Matt said, and sighed. "The whole séance was way more intense than I expected. We brought an actual fucking person into the world."

Ned greeted Matt and took his seat. "What are you two talking about?"

"I was just asking Mason about his evil twin," Matt said.

"He's not my twin," Mason said, scowling.

"Do you know why Christians believe one of a set of identical twins is evil?" Ned asked, leaning across Mason to talk to Matt. "It's because only one of them gets a soul, and the other one is just an empty shell, so it must be evil."

"That's insane," Matt said.

"Hey, I'm just the messenger," Ned said. "Identical twins come from one egg, so they must figure souls are assigned on a one-per-egg basis."

"So you can split an egg, but you can't split a soul?" Matt said.

Ned shrugged. "Ask the pastors and the bishops."

The house lights started to dim, and the crowd went quiet. Once it was completely dark, an eerie loop of soft green light floated onto the stage, stopping in the middle. After a few seconds a spotlight came on, illuminating a performer. She was wearing a necklace made of green glow sticks, and a lot of gold lamé—a snug top and leggings, a pleated gold skirt. Even her hair was gold. Everyone clapped politely when the beam revealed her, and she gestured for them to continue applauding, milking it to the max.

Eventually she launched into a monologue, talking about space—some of it sounding like scientific information, as if she were giving a presentation at a planetarium, but some of it was humorous, about aliens and abductions. It was almost stand-up comedy, Mason decided, but there were long stretches between the humorous parts, and at one point she just stood there, staring blankly, for what felt like way too long. Still, it was entertaining, and they laughed at the absurdity of it, clapping loudly when she left the stage.

As they waited in the dark, Matt leaned close, whispering, "She's conflating outer space with weirdness. Why do people think space is spacey? It's not, you know."

"Not to you," Mason said. "You're a scientist."

Peggy was the second act, although it took a moment to figure out that it was her as she walked onto the stage to polite applause. She was dressed as Dorothy from *The Wizard of Oz,* in the trademark sky-blue gingham dress and sparkly red shoes, but unlike Dorothy's simple braids, her pigtails stuck out wildly above her ears, one thicker than the other, wispy strands of hair escaping all around them. She wore thick glasses, distorting her eyes, and her mouth was full of metal—fake braces. She walked with a heavy gait, her shoulders hunched, and stopped in the middle of the stage, staring at the assembled crowd.

"I suppose you've been wondering what I've been up to since I got back to Kansas," she said finally, lisping through her mouth hardware. "Well, I've moved around a lot." With that she clomped over to the other side of the stage, her gait flat-footed and audible, disappearing from view in the wings and then returning a moment later, pushing a cardboard box so big it came up to her midriff. Stenciled on the front of the box was the admonition DON'T TOUCH MY STUFF.

Once it was positioned in the middle of the space, she folded open the top flaps and starting pulling things out of it—clothes, towels, junky plastic kitchen items like a colander and a soup ladle, old magazines, handfuls of loose paper in myriad colors—and threw them around the stage. There was a lot of stuff in that box, and it took her quite a while to empty it, briefly examining each item before tossing it, creating a cringe-inducing mess.

Returning to the wings, she came back with two smaller cardboard boxes and spent a few minutes picking up the junk littering the stage and stuffing it into one, then the other. Once they were loaded she stacked them on top of the larger box, but one of them tumbled to the floor, spilling its contents, and Peggy stood there, glaring at the tittering audience, as if it had been their fault.

It took her a few minutes to get everything back in the boxes, and stray sheets of paper and fabric still littered the stage, but stomping her feet and with great effort, she pushed the boxes offstage, and the lights fell; it was over.

They clapped for her in the dark room, and when Mason looked over at Ned, he had a huge smile on his face. Matt seemed impressed as well, clapping loudly, intermittently whistling through his fingers.

Immediately following Peggy came the third act, a woman in a leopard-print leotard banging on giant wind chimes, which took twice as long for the stage crew to set up as the actual performance.

After the three of them had taken a bow and the house lights went up again, Matt said, "Peggy was by far the best act."

"She was pretty funny," Ned agreed.

Matt wanted to talk to Peggy backstage, but Mason and Ned left, weaving through the boisterous crowd in the lobby.

Once they were in the car, Mason asked, "What did it mean, exactly?"

"I don't think it had any deep meaning," Ned said, watching for a break in the traffic and then turning onto the boulevard.

"It had to mean something."

"Well, maybe it was about hoarding, and the ephemeral nature of stuff. It winds up in boxes, wasting your time, slowing you down."

"She hates those TV shows, like *America's*

Filthiest People," Mason said. "You tried to get her to watch, remember, and she said it was exploitive and classist. And why was she dressed like Dorothy?"

"Maybe it was about status and social class. Dorothy went from her dirt-poor life to a place with shiny material wealth, but she chose to go back to Kansas because that's where her community was." He glanced over at Mason. "Or maybe the Dorothy outfit was the only thing in the prop closet that fit. Or maybe it was a critique of the cardboard-box industry. Who knows? Wasn't it just fun to watch?"

"Actually, it was," Mason admitted. He loved that about Ned, he realized—the loyalty. It didn't matter what Peggy did onstage, he valued it because it was her. They chatted about the evening, and once he let go of trying to understand the performances, it seemed a lot more entertaining.

Once they got home, Mason spent some time at his desk going through his research on Manuel, prepping for his excursion tomorrow, sliding the file into his backpack. He took a deep breath and connected to his bank to check on his credit card. Sam had been busy, with purchases at six different coffee places, a Mongolian barbecue joint, and several ride-share charges. There was a big purchase at Mr. Luthah's Menswear Meltdown in the Fashion District; that had to be the tux. It wasn't much more extravagant than what he'd spend on himself, he decided.

Ned stuck his head into the office. "Bart says he's free on Saturday."

"Great—I'll get him on the guest list."

"Don't you have to be up early?"

"Yeah. I'm leaving at six thirty."

"So come to bed," Ned said emphatically.

"Soon," Mason said, and pulled out his phone to text Bart's name to Val.

When he finally climbed into bed, Ned put his book down and cuddled up to him.

"So what exactly is a town car?" Mason asked, slipping his arm under Ned's neck.

"It's just a sedan with a roomy backseat. Like a taxi, only clean and comfortable. They're usually black."

"Henry's people are sending one for me in the morning."

Later, he found himself craning his neck to see Margaret, high above—she was walking on a tightrope, complete with a balance pole, her skirt billowing in the breeze. She took a tentative step, the balance pole swaying, and waved at Mason. She was wearing thick-lensed glasses, distorting her eyes, her smile revealing bands of dull gray metal. He hesitated, not wanting to distract her, but eventually decided to wave back.

Nine

It felt like the middle of the night when his alarm went off. The sky was light but the sun wasn't up yet, and thankfully Ned stayed asleep as Mason gingerly extracted himself from the bed.

After two pots of espresso and some muesli he crept back into the bedroom and quietly got dressed, then took a wad of cash from his desk and pulled on his backpack. When it was almost six thirty he looked out the front door, and there was the town car, black, just as Ned had predicted, waiting in front of the garage. The driver hopped out and opened the back door for him.

"Mr. Braithwaite?" he asked. He was older than Mason and wore a black suit.

"That's me," Mason said, and settled in. Ned was right—it was a lot nicer than a taxi.

Traffic was light, and the driver soon pulled onto the freeway. Mason got absorbed in his phone, checking his email, then reading the overnight news. Looking up at the city flashing past, he realized they were headed east.

"What airport are we going to?" he asked the driver.

"El Monte."

He knew of the town, but had no idea there was an airport there.

Soon they were off the freeway and in an industrial area—wide streets, low buildings, lots of parking out front. The driver pulled up in front of a nondescript business, then got out to open Mason's door.

"In there?" Mason asked dubiously.

"Yes, sir," he said.

It didn't look anything like an airport, although the sign over the door read FLIGHT SERVICES. Inside he found an office with a short counter and some lounge chairs. Almost as soon as he'd walked in, a young woman stepped up behind the counter and greeted him. Her hair was swept into a tight updo, and she wore a blouse with a stylized set of wings embroidered on it.

"Mr. Braithwaite?"

"You're the second person today who's pronounced my name correctly. I'm impressed."

She grinned. "I'm Nina. I just need to look at

an ID, and we'll be on our way."

He fished his driver's license out of his wallet and watched as she put it into a scanner and sat down for a minute, peering at a computer screen. With a few mouse clicks the scanner came to life, bright light leaking out around the cover. The copy must have been satisfactory, because she picked up his license and handed it back, then stepped around the counter.

"No bags?" she asked.

"Just my day pack."

"That's easy. If you'll follow me."

He didn't know what he'd been expecting, but when they pushed through the heavy doors at the end of the little office, they were outside on the tarmac. A shiny jet was waiting in front of them, its stairs down, the engines idling.

"No security check?" he asked Nina, raising his voice over the low whine of the turbines.

"That rule doesn't apply to small aircraft."

"It doesn't look small," he said. "It seems like a lot of airplane just for me."

"I'll be coming along too," she said.

A man in overalls with big orange headphones stood on the tarmac near the plane, watching them approach. Nina made some kind of hand signal to him, and he nodded, retreating toward the building.

Mason followed Nina up the stairs, stooping to enter the narrow space, where there were six very comfortable-looking seats.

"Sit anywhere you like," Nina said. He picked the second row.

The door to the cockpit was open, and momentarily a woman emerged, dressed like Nina but with a necktie and epaulets. She introduced herself as the pilot, Alison. "Nina will take good care of you," she said. "We'll be on our way soon."

And it was very soon—Alison went into the cockpit and closed the door, Nina pulled up the steps, and with that the engines revved up and the plane was moving. Lift-off seemed to happen fast, and at an absurdly sharp angle compared to a commercial flight.

"There's Wi-Fi if you need it," Nina said, pulling his attention away from the window. "Something to drink?"

"Maybe some water," he told her, and she soon returned with a bottle of Pellegrino, a glass, and a lemon wedge on a little tray. It felt so decadent. All this from Cyrus's gambling boat anchored off the coast. All this potential for travel at her disposal, and Margaret sat alone in her bedroom, looking out at the garden.

He watched as the mountains far below became desert, then pulled out his phone and did some reading. Nina interrupted him a while later.

"I wanted to give you the phone number for the local driver," she said.

"There's a car for me at that end?" he asked.

"Of course. Once you have a departure time in mind, just let the driver know, and he'll give us a heads-up."

"So you'll just be waiting around for me?" he asked.

She smiled. "That's our job."

Soon they started descending, and Mason looked out at the desert landscape, soon replaced by rippling bright white dunes stretching off to the horizon. White Sands, he realized, and then the complex of runways at Holloman Air Force Base came into view.

Minutes later the dry yellow landscape came up to meet them, much too quickly for comfort, but Alison touched down gently at the civilian airport, without any impact, just the sudden rumble of tarmac under the wheels. As soon as the plane stopped moving, Nina pushed the stairs down, and Mason stepped outside. The oven-like blast of heat made him inhale sharply, and he arched his back, happy to be standing erect once again. Another black town car pulled up as he descended the stairs. It had Texas plates, he noticed. Maybe the driver had come up from El Paso, as Mason had intended to do. He waved good-bye to Nina, and by the time he reached the car, the driver had jumped out to open the door for him. The guy was beefy and dark-haired, maybe in his thirties.

"I'm Omar," he said, a broad smile on his face. Once they were both sitting inside with the air-conditioning blasting, he asked, "Where are we headed?"

"It's a retirement home," Mason said, opening his backpack. "I have the address here somewhere."

"There are only a couple of those," Omar said. "Is it the VA?"

"I can't remember the name, but it's near a golf course."

"I know which one you mean. It's about fifteen minutes' drive."

Omar turned the car around and drove between two buildings, then through a security gate connected to the high fence around the airport. He didn't stop but nodded at the guard as the gate rolled open.

"Do you work for the Whitbys?" Mason asked him.

"I don't know that name," Omar said. "I'm contracted through the flight services company."

Omar turned onto a divided highway and headed for the town, the empty desert rolling by. It was flatter than the Mojave that Mason knew so well, and brighter. The quality of the light was different too—less red and brown, more white and yellow, he decided. The town was dusty and low-rise, he saw as they rolled into it, not run-down, exactly, but not prosperous, a hard-working type of community.

After a few minutes driving on city streets, Omar turned into the driveway of a long institutional building and stopped under a sunshade awning. This was the right place—Mason recognized it from the photos he'd seen on the website. He pulled on the handle to get out, but Omar jumped out and swung it open for him anyway.

"You don't have to get the door for me," he said. "It's too much."

"As you like," he said affably.

"I'm not sure how long I'll be."

"It doesn't really matter. I'll be nearby."

"I have your number," Mason said. "I guess I'll call when I'm ready?"

"Texting works too," he said, and climbed back into the driver's seat.

The lobby was plush, the cool air washing over him and giving him goosebumps. He stepped up to the reception desk and tried to sound as authoritative as he could.

"I'm here to see Manuel Whitby. Can you point me in the right direction?"

She frowned. "Mr. Whitby can't have visitors."

"I'm his cousin," Mason said sharply.

"Even so, it's absolutely impossible. I'm sorry."

"Why not?"

"I'm not going to discuss our patients with you."

"Can I talk to an administrator?"

"If you'd like. The director will be in after lunch. Her name is Mrs. Walsh."

Turning on his heel, he went back outside. The town car was gone, and he stood there for a minute under the sunshade, panting in the hot dry air. He hadn't anticipated getting shut down so quickly. He walked along the side of the building, its pebbly gravel planted with yuccas, thinking about his next move.

Around the corner he caught sight of a guy in nurse's scrubs sitting on a bench in the shade of the building, smoking a cigarette. Mason strolled toward him, trying to act nonchalant, even though there was no one else around.

"Hey," the nurse said, glancing up at him with a smile.

Small towns, Mason remembered, grinning to himself. He loved working in small towns. The people were predisposed to being friendly and sociable. He dropped onto the other end of the bench, trying to avoid the wafting smoke.

"Warm enough for you?" Mason asked.

The nurse snorted. "Come back in August."

"How did you know I'm not from here?"

He pointedly gave Mason the once-over. "I'd remember you."

"You can't know everyone in town."

"Maybe it's the shoes, then," he said, looking away and taking a drag.

Mason looked at his sneakers, unsure what about them would have given him away. "So what's it like to work here?"

"A grind. Like working anywhere."

"I get it," Mason said. "How would you like to make some cash on the side?"

He frowned, suspicious. "Doing what?"

"Sneak me inside to talk to my cousin."

"Who's your cousin?"

"Manuel Whitby."

He chuckled. "I could do that, but I'd be

ripping you off."

"Why do you say that?"

"Manuel has advanced Alzheimer's. You could talk to him, but he wouldn't talk back. I suppose you could come back at dusk and watch him get agitated, but it's not pretty."

"Damn it," Mason said. What a freaking waste of jet fuel. How many tons of carbon had been spewed over the Southwest to bring him here, just for him to find out what they wouldn't tell him on the phone—that Manuel wasn't able to talk to him?

"Have you spoken to David?" the nurse asked, pulling his attention back.

"Right—David," Mason said. "I forgot about him."

"Funny how you didn't know Manuel had Alzheimer's, and you haven't spoken to his husband. I mean, you being his cousin, and all."

"We were never that close. I don't have David's number."

"There you go," he said, stubbing out his cigarette in the gravel. "Now we have some billables."

"What?"

"I'll sell you that piece of information. David's number."

Mason studied him for a moment. "Did you ever hear of the idea that information wants to be free?"

"If it were freely available, you'd already have it," he said. "Besides, you're the one who started talking about money."

"I did, didn't I." Mason sighed. "How much do you want?" As soon as he'd said it, he winced. What a foolish way to start a negotiation.

"Fifty bucks."

"How about twenty?"

"Forty, and I'll go in right now and get it for you."

"Fine," Mason said flatly.

The nurse stood and held out his palm.

"Cash on delivery, man," Mason said, scowling at him.

Without a word he stepped inside the building, the security door clicking shut behind him. Maybe it wasn't a wasted journey, if he could talk to David. He'd been with Manuel a long time—maybe he'd be able to explain the discrepancies in Margaret's letters.

He breathed in the dry air, filling his lungs. Even though it was crazy hot, it wasn't stifling, more like a dry sauna. It felt good to breathe deeply, and he closed his eyes, focusing on that for a while, the only sound the hum of distant air-conditioning machinery.

The nurse came back, a yellow sticky note in hand, and said, "Got it."

Mason stood, pulling a wad of cash out of his pocket and peeling off the agreed-on sum, exchanging it for the sticky note. Glancing at it, he saw that it did indeed have a phone number on it.

"What else can you tell me about David?" Mason asked.

"He lives somewhere in town, and comes by a few times a week."

"Is he the same age as Manuel?"

"Yeah, super old. But he has all his marbles, and he drives—a sweet little Mercedes."

"Thanks," Mason said, and pulled out his phone.

"So what do you want with Manuel, when you obviously don't even know him?"

"I could explain all that," Mason said, "but it would cost you forty bucks."

He grinned, and stepped toward the door. "Be gentle with David. He's a nice guy."

Once he'd gone inside, Mason glanced around to make sure he was alone, and dialed David's number. Thankfully, he picked up.

"I'm working for a relative of Manuel's," Mason explained. "His second cousin Margaret Whitby, from Los Angeles. Can we talk?"

"I remember that name," David said slowly. "I'm afraid Manny isn't himself anymore."

"I know he has Alzheimer's," Mason said. "I was sorry to hear that. It must be incredibly diffi-cult for you."

"You have no idea."

"Perhaps I could talk to you, in lieu of talking to Manuel."

"What exactly did you want from him?" David said.

"Margaret wanted to clarify a couple things. Nothing dramatic, and nothing about money, I promise. I won't take too much of your time. I'm in town—maybe I could buy you lunch?"

"All right. I'm headed to the golf course—meet me at the clubhouse around noon."

"Hell, yes," Mason said after he'd hung up.

He texted Omar, and by the time he'd put his phone away and walked back to the front of the building, the car was pulling up the driveway. Mason opened the door and climbed in, happy that Omar didn't try to jump out to assist.

"I have a meeting later at the golf course clubhouse," he said. "Before that, is there a decent coffee place nearby?"

"Independent coffeehouse, I'm thinking, rather than a chain, correct?"

"If there's a good one," Mason said.

"There is."

As Omar pulled down the driveway, Mason leaned over the seat. "How did you know I was an indie coffee guy?"

Omar laughed. "Corporate types who travel a lot want the predictability of the chains. You don't seem like that."

He spent the rest of the morning at the coffeehouse, nursing a quadruple espresso.

Back on the street, he met Omar and climbed into the welcome air-conditioned interior.

"Great pick," Mason said. "I'm surprised to find such a funky place in such a small town."

"Never underestimate a small town," Omar said. "So where to?"

"The golf course."

"The public one or the private one?"

"I have no idea. It has a restaurant."

"That's the private club. It's not far."

They pulled up at a luxe low-slung building, and Mason climbed out.

"I should be about an hour," he said, stooping to look in at Omar.

"You know I don't have anything else to do, right? I'm working for you today, so you don't have to worry about inconveniencing me."

"I get it," Mason said. "I'm not used to this kind of service."

"Just relax and enjoy it. Make some demands if you need to."

Mason nodded. "How about this: I don't know how long I'll be, and you'd damn well better be here when I'm through."

Omar guffawed. "I've had lots of clients like that too."

The restaurant was just off the lobby of the clubhouse, and as he strode in and looked around the space, a diminutive gray-haired man sitting against the wall beckoned him over.

"Mr. Braithwaite?" he asked as Mason approached his table, rising partway from his seat. "David Schaffer." He was well coiffed and wore a golf shirt, but he looked tired.

"Don't get up," Mason said, and pulled out a chair. "How did you know it was me?"

"People don't usually walk in here looking lost.

And you're not dressed for golf."

Before Mason sat, he found a business card in his pocket and handed it across the table.

"A psychic," David said, reading the card and looking up, his eyes growing wide. "Why does Margaret Whitby need a psychic?"

The waitress interrupted them, greeting David by name. He ordered a steak, still holding Mason's card.

"Do you have anything green?" Mason asked, not bothering to look at a menu. "Maybe a plain salad?"

"Of course," she said, jotting it down.

"And guacamole, if you have that. And fries on the side."

"A hungry psychic," David said, grinning faintly, once she'd gone. He set Mason's business card carefully on the table in front of him.

"I've been doing some research for Margaret," Mason said, "and I came across some correspondence she had with Manuel. Most of the letters dated back twenty years or more, but two of them came from Manuel earlier this year. They were sent from Spain."

David shook his head. "That's impossible. We haven't been back to Spain for decades, and Manny hasn't even been able to write a letter for many years."

"I wondered about that."

He studied Mason for a moment. "Why are the California Whitbys looking for Manny now?"

Mason hesitated. Henry had asked him to keep the whole story under wraps, but it was unlikely David would talk to anybody who could embarrass Henry in the media, and right now showing his cards was the best way to get what he needed from David.

"A man showed up at Margaret's house claiming to be Manuel. I'm trying to figure out what's going on."

"Manny is at a care facility here in town. I can assure you he's not visiting Los Angeles. He isn't capable of it."

Mason pulled out his phone and found the photo he'd taken of Etor. "This is the guy. Does he look anything like Manuel?"

"Not even remotely," David said, peering at the image. "He looks thirty years younger."

Mason tucked his phone back in his pocket.

"He's a liar, if he says he's Manny," David said. "Will he be arrested?"

"I'm not sure how it'll play out," Mason said. Even if Manuel hadn't written those letters, it didn't mean the rest of Etor's story wasn't true.

Their food arrived, and Mason tucked into his salad as David methodically cut up his steak.

"So what are the California Whitbys like?" David asked.

"Rich," Mason said through a mouthful of lettuce. "Old money. A little eccentric. There are gay people in that lineage too—Margaret's son, for one. If I wasn't already with someone, I'd be all over him."

David laughed. "How long have you been with your guy?"

"About four years."

"Maybe you're feeling the itch of infidelity."

"I hope not. How long have you been with Manuel?"

"Over forty years," David said, a wistful look in his eye. "I grew up in the Northeast. Manny and I moved to Alamogordo for my work. We had a good life here, and we both love the desert. Things got difficult as Manny's health declined. The last straw was when the house got robbed." He scowled at the memory. "I moved Manny into assisted living, and I downsized."

"What got stolen?" Mason asked, eyeing him.

"Everything—electronics, furniture, silver. They even rifled my file cabinet."

"What kind of work do you do here? It's such a small town."

"I'm retired," David said, setting down his fork and leaning back. "I was with the government."

"At Holloman base?"

"Something like that," he said, his gaze settling on Mason.

"They threw gay people out of the military until very recently," Mason said, dipping a corn chip into his guac. "You couldn't have been out to them."

"I wasn't enlisted," David said, his tone guarded now.

"It's not anything I need to know, but I am curious. Is it a secret or something? I've read about

Holloman. Eisenhower met with aliens there in the fifties, and saucers used to land there all the time." He held up his palms. "Allegedly."

David looked surprised. "You're quite the character."

"Fringe phenomena is my field, and Holloman is significant in that world. Did you ever meet any aliens? I haven't, but I've seen them."

David chuckled, his eyes bright. "Even if I'd flown to Zeta Reticuli myself, I couldn't tell you about it."

"That's oddly specific," Mason said, pushing aside his plate. He leaned closer and spoke quietly. "Did you actually do that?"

David shook his head, smirking at the idea.

"What about people crossing over from parallel universes—showing up one day with a passport from a country that doesn't exist. Did you ever run across that?"

"That's even farther out than Eisenhower meeting the grays."

Mason's eyes narrowed. "Who said it was the grays?"

The waitress dropped the check on the table, and Mason picked it up, pulling out his wad of cash and peeling off some bills.

"I said I'd buy," he explained. "Can I give Margaret your number once this nonsense is straightened out?"

"Of course," David said. "I'd be happy to speak with her."

Mason thanked him and walked back into the lobby, where he texted Omar. It felt good to have another piece of it, an explanation for what had become of Margaret's cousin in this world. It was what he'd come all this way to find out. But there was more work to do, and that was back in LA.

Climbing into the town car when it pulled up, he told Omar, "One more stop—that coffee place again—and then I'm ready to go back to Los Angeles."

"I'll let the flight crew know," Omar said, and took a few seconds to thumb-type a text before pulling away.

At the coffeehouse the barista remembered Mason, greeting him with a friendly "Howdy, stretch." When Mason ordered a quadruple espresso, his expression shifted to disbelief. "You just had one of those. Won't you get jittery?"

Mason had to laugh. "Dude—don't go discouraging your clientele."

He drank the coffee on the drive to the airport. Omar rolled down the rear window as they pulled up to the security gate. The guard asked Mason for his ID, but after a perfunctory glance at it they were waved through. As the town car pulled up near the waiting plane, Nina started to lower the stairs.

Before he climbed out, he asked Omar, "Should I be tipping you?"

"Don't even go there," he said, holding up his hand. "I can't accept it."

"Well, thanks for all the driving."

"I'll see you again soon."

"You bet," Mason said, and climbed out.

Nina welcomed him as he walked up the stairs into the jet.

"How about some water?" she asked. "It's hot out there."

"Sure," he said, and minutes later watched as the ground fell away below them. He pulled out his pad and made notes on what he'd learned about Manuel, and his meeting with David, then read through it again, getting it clear in his mind.

When they were back on the ground again at El Monte, Nina thanked him politely and told him the car would be waiting for him on the street outside the office. It looked the same as the one he'd been in this morning, and the same as Omar's car. The driver, however, was new.

He held the door open for Mason, then asked politely, "Destination?"

Mason rattled off his home address, and they were able to cut through the heavy Friday traffic in the carpool lane. On the way Mason sent Henry a brief text.

Back from NM. Got what I needed. Thanks for arranging it.

Climbing out in front of his house, he thanked the driver and went inside. It felt surreal to be home again so quickly: the familiar greenery on the street, the hazy gray light, the comparatively humid air.

"You're back," Ned said, coming out of the

office. "How did it go?"

"Great—I got some questions answered. Are you still working?"

"Nah. Sit and tell me about it."

He stretched out on the sofa with Ned, who pulled off Mason's socks and massaged his bare feet.

"What kind of plane was it?"

"I don't know. A shiny one. There were six recliners inside, and just me. I had my own flight attendant." Mason closed his eyes. "It's a whole different world, having those resources."

"The money makes life easier," Ned said, "but it doesn't make them any happier than you and me. I also think it makes them crazier, because they hear 'no' less often. 'You want a pet chimp, and a theme park, and a new nose? Sure, we can do that.'"

"That actually describes the Whitbys pretty well. The matriarch hangs out in her room all day because she can."

"So Gilbert called," Ned said, his tone becoming more serious. "He thought he saw you on TV today."

"In New Mexico?"

"In Brentwood. He thought you were using a pseudonym, because the caption read 'Sam Rutherford.'"

"Oh, god." The surname was familiar—an old family name, he remembered, somewhere on his mother's side.

"What was Sam doing in Brentwood?" Ned asked.

"How would I know? Why was he on TV?"

"It's on the station's website," Ned said, and got up to get his tablet, sitting next to Mason when he got back and starting the video.

The reporter was standing on a street with pleasant bungalows and drought-tolerant landscaping, an expensive-looking maroon-colored sedan filling the frame behind her.

"A bizarre story in Brentwood tonight," she explained, even though it was broad daylight, deep concern in her eyes. "High-voltage electric lines fell onto a car driven by controversial real estate developer Douglas Grankin, trapping him in the car for several hours while fire crews worked to rescue him. A passerby describes the horrifying scene."

The video cut to Sam, speaking into a foam-capped mike with the TV station's logo on the base. Mason felt his heartbeat accelerate.

"I can't believe he was smart enough not to get out of the car," Sam said. "He just sat there. If he'd stepped out, he would have been fried like a chalupa."

"Were you able to warn him to stay inside the vehicle?" the reporter asked off-camera.

"Nah," Sam said, sounding disheartened. "Maybe someone else did."

"Did you see what caused the wires to fall?"

"I don't know anything about that," Sam said.

Ned paused the video. "He does the same thing with his eyebrows that you do when you're lying. Watch the eyes," he said, and started the video again, jumping back a few seconds.

Sam knotted his eyebrows and squinted slightly before he made the denial. Ned paused the video again.

"It's like he's trying to be extra convincing using his eyes."

"I do not do that when I lie," Mason said.

"Yeah, you do," Ned said, and pressed PLAY.

"I saw that dummy sitting there for hours, shouting at the firefighters," Sam continued, waving his arms for emphasis. "He has no manners. They were trying to help him, and he's screaming at them like they were his own personal city councilors. You know, like the ones he's purchased." He looked into the camera meaningfully.

The video cut to a firefighter in baggy yellow pants pulling open the car door, and Grankin stepping out, angry and red-faced, holding his palm up to the camera lens.

"EMTs tell us that Grankin refused medical attention and was unable to restart his car, which likely suffered extensive electronic damage due to the high voltage," the reporter explained, the camera on her once again. "Grankin also refused an interview and has since left the scene. Back to you in the studio."

"Isn't it weird that you know that guy?" Ned said.

"Grankin? I wouldn't say I really know him. But yeah, it's definitely a small world."

"Mason, look at me," Ned said gravely. "Did

you ask Sam to go after him?"

"You know me better than that. I was upset at the way Grankin treated me, but I'd never try to fry him."

"Would Sam?"

"I can't believe that," he said, although the nauseous feeling in his stomach said otherwise. "I'll have a word with him, though, if it'll put your mind at ease."

"Good," Ned said. He seemed relieved. "I know it sounds crazy, but crazy things happen to you all the time."

A set of keys rattled in the lock at the front door, and Peggy came in, dressed for the office.

"Hey, boys," she said. "I just sorted out the details of the garden party gig. It's amazing—we're all getting paid scale."

"I take it scale is a good thing?" Mason asked.

"It means a fair wage. It's extremely rare for musicians to get paid well."

"Who's 'we'?" Ned asked.

"Me and the band. I lined up four musicians: drums, guitar, upright bass, and xylophone."

"Xylophone?" Mason asked.

"It's appropriate to the genre," Peggy said. "I'm so happy I don't have to pay them out of my own pocket, or worse, ask them to work for free, and then owe them each a favor. Your friend Val said the Whitbys wanted everyone to get properly paid."

"I spoke to Val today too," Ned said. "She seemed nice."

"Are you getting paid?" Peggy asked.

"Minimum wage, but yeah, it was nice of her to offer."

"We'll have to coordinate party tactics," Mason said.

"After we eat," Peggy said. "Do we have a plan for dinner?"

Ned said, "I was thinking teriyaki tofu."

"Let me get changed, and I'll help you," she said, and went down the hall.

While they were cooking, Mason spent some time at his desk, planning what each of his crew would be doing at the party. Sam had to be visible in the garden as Mason, and Ned and Peggy would act as lookouts.

At dinner they talked about Peggy's performance last night, congratulating her on the originality. She explained a little about her inspiration for the piece, but that didn't give Mason any insight into the meaning, and he decided not to ask. As Ned had suggested, maybe it was enough just to have enjoyed it. Mason told her about his trip to New Mexico, and Ned told her about Sam briefing the media after the power lines fell on Douglas Grankin's car.

She looked at Mason, shocked at the story. "Should we be worried?"

"I'll talk to him," he said, and stood up, ending the discussion by starting to clear the table.

When they'd finished cleaning up, Ned perched on the sofa. "Tell us what we should be doing at the party."

"It's pretty straightforward," Mason said, sitting on the other wing. "Keep an eye on Etor, and if he goes into the house, text me."

"Val knows that I'm supposed to be watching the guests," Peggy said, joining them. "So the stage will have a good view, but I won't be able to follow the guy. When I'm onstage, I don't think I'll be able to pull out my phone to text you either."

"I'll be circulating," Ned said, "so I'll be able to keep an eye on him. Will you have amplification for the music?"

"Mikes and speakers, the whole nine yards. It won't be loud, though—Val says Henry wants it to be just background entertainment."

"Instead of texting, maybe you could use a code phrase if you see Etor go into the house," Ned said.

"Great idea," Mason said. "Something that'll alert me, but won't tip off Etor."

"How about 'Greek coffee'?" Peggy said.

Mason chuckled. "Where did that come from?"

"It won't come up in any of the songs," she said.

"It works—it's odd enough that I'm sure I'll notice it."

"I'll look forward to hearing you work that into your routine," Ned said. "And what does this guy look like, anyway?"

Mason pulled out his phone and found the photo he'd taken of Etor, handing it to Ned, who studied it for a moment, then passed it to Peggy.

"He'll be easy enough to spot in a crowd," she said. "I'm sure none of your blue-blood clients slick their hair back like that."

"I wish Sam was here to coordinate with us," Ned said.

"At least his role is easy," Peggy said. "He just has to be visible, and we know he's skilled at doing that."

"I suppose he'll come by tomorrow to pick up his tux," Ned said.

"He won't miss the party," Mason said. "Of that, I'm certain."

Later, in the dream world, he found himself in Omar's car, in the back, although Omar was nowhere to be seen. He had his feet up on the seat, his arms tightly around his knees, trying not to touch anything but the upholstery under him. Outside the windows he could see bright blue sparks arcing in the dark, the car surrounded by them, energized with electricity.

Forcing himself to wake up, he thought about writing it down on his bedside notepad, but decided to let it go. Instead he made sure his mind was clear enough that he wouldn't fall back into it, the feeling of danger, the fear.

Ten

For the second time this week he awoke to Ned's bemused face, gently shaking his shoulder.

"Billy's on his way over," he said.

Ned had already started the espresso machine, and Mason sat at the kitchen counter to munch on half a grapefruit and some blackberries.

"Where's Peggy?" he asked.

"Rehearsing, I assume," Ned said, pouring the pot of espresso into a cup and sliding it over to Mason.

"She said she didn't need to rehearse," he said irritably.

"Well, then maybe she's getting the band's gear

lined up. Does it matter?"

"I want things to go smoothly tonight."

"Let her worry about her part. Things will go better if you try not to be a control freak."

Mason grunted, sipping at his espresso. There was probably some truth in that, but he wasn't lucid enough to process the idea, let alone argue about it.

"So am I paying Billy, or is it a favor?" he asked.

"It's his work, and you need it for a job. I think you have to pay him."

"How much?"

"Ask him."

Billy arrived soon after, greeting them loudly with air kisses near both cheeks. Unlike the nights he performed, today he was dressed plainly, in jeans and a rugby shirt, although the man bag he had slung over his shoulder was pocked with decorative silver studs. His black hair was perfectly styled to look unkempt, and he wore a little bit of eye makeup, but for Billy this was as stripped-down as it got.

"Ned told me a little about the look you're working," he said, tilting Mason's chin down to inspect his face.

"Nondescript," Mason said. "I have to blend in at a garden party with a bunch of corporate types. I'm going to wear my gray suit."

"All those words," Billy said, closing his eyes and massaging his temples, "make me sad."

"You're so good at turning ducklings into swans," Ned said. "I'm sure you can do the opposite too."

"We're not exactly starting with a swan," he

said dubiously, giving Mason the once-over. "But I can try. I know we only have a few hours."

"Like, eight or nine," Mason said.

"Oh, god," Billy said, his eyes growing wide. "Then we'd better get going."

"Where?" Mason asked.

"You'll need a wig. There's no time to dye that rusted-out mop."

"Fine," Mason said, ignoring the dis. "Let's go."

"Don't you need to change?" Billy said, glancing at Mason's T-shirt and shorts.

"To go shopping?" Mason said sharply, and Ned stifled a laugh.

Billy shrugged. "Suit yourself."

They climbed into Billy's little Fiat, Mason's knees brushing the dashboard even with the seat pushed all the way back. It was a car for driving the Amalfi coast, not navigating this town.

"Do you park this thing under your bed?" Mason asked.

Billy snorted and pulled a tight U-turn, tearing down the street, steering hard, weaving around the traffic whenever he could get a speed advantage. It was nerve-wracking, but they didn't have far to go. Billy pulled into a strip-mall parking lot and climbed out of the car.

Mason followed him toward the shop, BRENDA'S WIG WORLD in tall red letters above the door. "Who's Brenda?" he asked.

"The name is made up. It's Mrs. Lee's shop. I think she's Korean."

Billy pulled the door open, and an elderly woman came over, cheerfully greeting him by name. She was obviously wearing one of her own products, swept up in a beehive with a mesh of decorative rhinestones at one side. Mason had to admit it looked pretty amazing.

Billy introduced him, explaining, "Mrs. Lee is the best in the business."

"You flatter me," she said, clearly pleased. And to Mason, "He likes my shop because I give him a volume discount."

"We need something long enough to cover Mason's hair," Billy said. "But not too long. And black—very black."

Mrs. Lee studied Mason thoughtfully, like a surgeon planning a complex procedure, then nodded and went into the back of the shop.

While she was gone, Billy said, "You're so fair, we have to go black."

"You're the expert," Mason said, resigned to whatever was about to happen.

Mrs. Lee returned with a shaggy-looking mass of black hair, and with Billy's help, they pulled it onto Mason's head, then stood back to assess the look.

"It's dramatic," Mrs. Lee said, folding her arms. "He looks like a ghost."

"I'll fix that with makeup," Billy said.

"It's kind of getting in my eyes," Mason said, pawing at the bangs.

"Don't worry about that," Billy said. "It's an easy fix. Does it fit?"

"I guess it feels OK."

Billy fiddled with the hair around Mason's ears for a minute, then stood back. "Sold," he said finally, and yanked it off his head, plopping it unceremoniously on the counter.

"Cash or plastic?" Mrs. Lee asked, and Billy looked at Mason expectantly.

"Right," Mason said, and scrambled to pull his wad of cash from his pants. "How much?"

"Thirty-nine, plus tax," she said, ringing it up at the cash register.

He had to grin at the price; he'd expected it to cost many times that much. "You know how to find a bargain," he said to Billy.

"Please," he said. "I could put on a floor show with a half yard of chiffon and a bottle of nail polish. This is what I do."

They returned to Mason's place in the Fiat, Billy's lead foot making for a white-knuckle ride.

"Let me get my makeup kit," Billy said after he'd parked, then lifted a large wheelie suitcase out of the back of the car, pulling out its collapsible handle.

Mason looked at the bag suspiciously as Billy maneuvered it over the threshold. He gestured down the hall. "Should we work in the bathroom?"

"Too small. We'll use the kitchen."

He had Mason perch on a stool, then set his case flat on the kitchen floor and zipped it open, first setting up two work lights, the kind painters use in empty apartments, at either end of the counter.

"Don't squint," Billy said, adjusting the angle of the lamps so the glare was aimed at Mason's head.

"It's so bright."

"Suck it up," Billy demanded.

He pulled the wig onto Mason's head, adjusting it carefully, and then pulled out his barber tools, snipping away at the bangs. Mason screwed his eyes shut, then looked again when he heard the front door open. Billy stopped cutting as Ned came in.

"Where were you?" Mason asked.

"I had to pick up my uniform at Val's." He held up a plastic shopping bag.

"Is it a loaner, or did you have to buy it?" Billy asked.

"I bought it, but it wasn't outrageously expensive."

"You're being such a good sport," Mason said. "I'm sorry to put you through all this."

"It'll be entertaining," Ned said, stepping over to watch Billy groom the wig. "I'm liking the brunette thing. Are you going to fix his face?"

"Of course," Billy said.

"What's wrong with my face?"

"It's not designed for dark hair," Billy said. "You look like someone cranked the contrast up to ten."

Ned chuckled. "I guess I'm not going to be doing any cooking today."

"Until further notice, this is an atelier of creative beauty," Billy said.

Ned snorted and went down the hall.

Billy stepped back, assessing his work. He held up a hand mirror and asked, "What do you think?"

"Damn," Mason said, craning to take in the overall effect. Tousled dark locks covered his forehead and the tops of his ears. "It looks really natural. I should wear this every day."

"Let's not get carried away," Billy said, raising his eyebrows and taking away the mirror. "Before I do the makeup, I'll need to see what you're wearing."

Mason got up and brushed the synthetic black hair off himself, then went to the bedroom closet and pulled out his suit. It was the only thing he owned that fit him really well, as it had been tailor-made by some scientists he'd worked with on a case. They had access to futuristic materials that never seemed to wrinkle or pick up dirt. He hung the gray jacket in the kitchen doorway, draping the necktie he always wore with it, a hibiscus print in olive green, over one of the shoulders. Billy examined it, feeling the fabric of the sleeve.

"Nice material, but the boringness is making my eyelids droop."

"It's vintage 1952," Mason said. "Besides, I want to blend in tonight, not stand out."

"What were you saying?" he asked. "I drifted off, because I got so bored."

Mason sat on the stool again. "What kind of makeup job are you going to do?"

"Extremely subtle," Billy said, stooping to dig through his case.

Ned came out of the office. "Are you doing his

makeup? You have to use waterproof stuff, or he'll smudge it."

"I'm not nine years old," Mason protested.

Billy rose and hovered over his eyes with an ominous-looking metal tool. "Hold perfectly still," he said. "One wrong move and you'll be blind."

"Jesus, man," Mason protested, but he froze, trying not to blink.

Billy worked on his eyes, manipulating the lids for what felt like a very long time. Ned sat on one of the other stools, watching.

"Every hair on your body is exactly the same color," Billy said, as if it were a source of frustration.

"I call it electric orange," Ned said.

Careful not to move his head, Mason said quietly, "I blame my parents."

Billy stepped back, and Ned leaned in, examining him. "Wow, that's amazing."

"Can I see?" Mason asked.

"Not yet."

"You should give him a smoky eye," Ned said.

"What is that?" Mason asked. "I don't think I want that."

Billy chuckled. "It's hard enough just getting to 'nondescript.'"

Ned wandered off, and Billy worked on Mason's eyebrows, brushing something cold into them. Then, with brushes and pads, and several different shades of powder and tubes, he did the rest of his face, working up to his hairline and down to his shirt collar. He studied Mason intently, then moved the lights around and had Mason turn his head. After a few minutes touching up his nose with a sponge pad, he stood back, looking satisfied.

"I think we're there," he said, and stooped to pull an oversize aerosol can out of his case. "Hold still, and close your eyes. Don't breathe until I say so."

"What are you going to do?" Mason asked, eyeing the spray can.

"It's to keep the makeup in place. This way it won't run if you get sweaty. Even so, you shouldn't touch it."

Mason held his breath while Billy sprayed, trying not to flinch at the distressing sensation of viscous liquid adhering to his skin.

"OK, breathe," Billy said. "And open your eyes."

His eyelashes felt like they were gummed shut, but he managed to pull them open.

"It takes a minute to dry," Billy said, dabbing delicately at the side of Mason's neck with his finger. He positioned the wig on his head once again, then stepped back and pulled out his phone, snapping several photos of Mason, straight on and from both sides.

"Give me a mirror," Mason said.

"We'll go to your bedroom," he said. "But first, put on the suit. You want the full effect."

Mason dropped his shorts, not shy in front of Billy, and donned the suit pants, then pulled on the suit jacket over his T-shirt.

"When you go in the bedroom, look at yourself from across the room, in low light, because that's how people are going to see you. It won't look so realistic close up under harsh lighting, but out-doors, in the evening light, you're a different man."

Mason walked down the hall and stood in front of the floor mirror, stunned at what he saw. It was almost as weird as when his reflection had started talking back to him, seeing this man wearing his clothes who only bore a passing resemblance to him. This person had a dark complexion, and his nose was smaller than his own.

"Who are you?" he asked the mirror.

"You like?" Billy asked, standing behind him.

"It's freaking strange to look at, but it's perfect. It's exactly what I need."

Ned came in and stood behind him, looking at Mason in the mirror. "Billy, you're a genius."

Mason took a closer look at his face. His nose looked smaller because of the way Billy had layered different shades of makeup, darker on the sides. The eyebrows looked fake at close range, and there were dark lines painted along his eyelids. His skin had a sheen to it, the way legs looked through nylon stockings. When he bared his teeth and stretched his mouth, though, the surface didn't crack or pucker, retaining its pliability.

"How did you turn my eyelashes black?" he asked.

Billy laughed. "Trade secret. Remember, don't touch anything."

"So what do I owe you?" Mason asked, stepping out of the bathroom.

"Well," he began, "with the thirty percent family discount …"

"That's not necessary. It's business."

"I am kind of exhausted, and this is highly skilled work. Two fifty?"

"That I can do," Mason said, and went into the office to get the cash. "So how do I get it off later?" he asked as he handed it over.

Billy pocketed the bills, looking concerned. "A long hot shower. It's so tragic to think of all that work washing away."

"At least you got photos," Mason said, and saw him to the door.

Ned emerged a minute later in his waiter's uniform: black pants and black vest over a white shirt, with a little black bowtie.

"You look good," Mason said. "It's kind of snug. It emphasizes your hotness."

"It has to be. You don't want loose fabric to snag on stuff when you're working."

"You look too suave to be a waiter. I feel like I should spill ketchup on your vest or something to repel the lusty boys."

Ned laughed. "I don't suppose there'll be many of those at the Whitbys' garden party."

The front door opened, and Sam came in, wearing a loose tank top and uncomfortably tight jeans.

"Come on in," Ned said.

Not catching the sarcasm, Sam said, "Thanks,"

then turned to Mason. "Whoa—great makeover. You don't look anything like me anymore."

"It's weird, right?" Mason said.

"Dude—it's perfect."

"We saw you interviewed on the local news," Ned said, his brow furrowing. "What a coincidence that you were in Brentwood to witness that accident. You know that guy gave Mason a hard time, right?"

Sam looked thoughtful. "I guess he might have told me that, but I must have tuned it out." He leaned toward Ned and said conspiratorially, "So much drama with this one, am I right?"

"So it was just a freak accident," Ned said.

Sam shrugged. "What else?"

Ned studied him for a second, then said, "I'm going to grab my phone so you can photograph us."

Once Ned had gone down the hall, Mason said under his breath, "Did you have something to do with that accident?"

"I'm hurt that you'd think that," Sam said, coolly holding his gaze. "Is it my fault the electric company strings up their wires with crappy insulators that fail in the first stiff breeze?"

"You seem to know a lot about it."

"The guy's fine—what's the big deal? He had a good scare, which is what he did to us. Balance has been restored to the universe."

"Those are quite the pants," Ned said as he came back.

"They're not mine. I borrowed them from a friend."

"What friend?" Mason demanded.

"A gentleman caller. He's a PMT—one of those acronyms, anyway."

"You mean an EMT?"

"Maybe. He was pretty hot."

Ned grinned. "And just a couple sizes smaller than you. Can you take our photo?"

Sam took his phone and held it up toward them, peering at the screen. Ned stood next to Mason, wrapping an arm around his waist and pulling him close.

"Say 'deception,'" Sam said, and the flash flickered a few times.

"Should we do a three-way selfie?" Ned asked.

"No," Sam and Mason said simultaneously.

"Listen," Sam said, handing the phone back to Ned. "Can you give me my tux? I have to get going."

"I'll get it," Ned said, and went down the hall.

"You're not coming with me?" Mason asked. "Should I be concerned?"

"Don't worry—I'll be there. It's what you created me for, bruh."

"Bruh? You sound like a frat boy."

"And you look like a CPA," Sam said harshly.

"Good," Mason snapped.

"Why are you guys arguing?" Ned said, returning with the garment bag.

"It's just stage fright," Sam said, taking the hanger loop in hand. "So when I get to the gate, am I me, or am I you?"

"Give them my name," Mason said. "I'll use yours."

"Later," Sam said, stepping toward the door.

"Can I at least tell you the plan?" Mason called after him.

Sam turned back and took a deep breath, as if it took all his energy to muster the patience for this. "Make sure Etor thinks you're outside when you go into the house. No Mason-splaining required."

"And text me if he goes inside, or if you lose sight of him."

"Easy peasy."

"Do you have my phone number, at least?"

Sam arched his eyebrows. "Oh, I've got your number, toots," he said, and was gone.

After the door closed behind him, Ned said, "He's so odd."

"At least he had nothing to do with the wires falling on Grankin's car. I asked."

"And you believe him?"

Mason nodded vigorously, trying not to squint the way Sam had done on TV. "Unequivocally."

"If you say so," Ned said dubiously. "I need to go," he said, glancing at his phone. "I'm helping the food guys unload the van, and I have to meet them at Clementine Manor."

"I guess I'll see you there," Mason said. "Don't kiss me—it'll muss my makeup."

Ned grinned. "I never thought I'd hear you say those words." He stood there for a minute, examining Mason. "I definitely like you better as a redhead."

"I'm glad to hear it."

Before he left, Ned said, "Eat something before you go. And don't touch your face."

It was still a few hours until the party started, so Mason carefully pulled off the wig and took off the suit. Setting an alarm on his phone, he stretched out on the sofa, hoping to psych himself up for the evening rather than to fall asleep. He had to stop himself repeatedly from itching his nose or rubbing his eyes. He spent a few minutes breathing slowly, quelling his thoughts, inducing a trance state.

The alarm startled him awake what felt like moments later. Putting the wig back on, he adjusted it in the bathroom mirror, making sure none of his real hair was visible. It took a few minutes to get dressed, finding a white shirt and tying his necktie, dusting off his oxfords. He checked the overall effect in the floor mirror, and marveled at how different he looked—the way the black hair fell suited his face, and even close up, his darker skin looked natural. Billy had extended the makeup well below his shirt collar, smoothly obscuring any trace of his naturally pasty flesh. This had better be worth the effort.

Pulling out his phone, he summoned a rideshare. No way could he cycle all the way to Clementine Manor and still look presentable. As it was, he hoped it would be cooler in the hills. It was almost too warm to wear a jacket, and even though Billy had spray-glued everything in place, he didn't want his fake face to slough off with sweat. By the time the car arrived, he'd decided to carry his jacket until he got there.

The driver greeted him amicably before pulling out and heading toward the freeway, glancing at him in the rearview mirror only once. Even though twilight was just descending, he didn't seem to notice Mason's paint job. Billy was good, he realized.

The gate to Clementine Manor stood open when the driver pulled up, with a uniformed guard standing next to the intercom box. The driver rolled down the rear window, and Mason eyed the guard.

"Sam Braithwaite," he said, using the name he'd given Val for the list.

The guard swiped at his phone, studying it intently for a second, then nodded. "Drop-off is in front of the garage," he told the driver, and to Mason, "The event is through the house."

It was a relief that he had only given Mason a perfunctory glance, hadn't seen anything odd in him. Apparently the makeup job didn't look as obvious as it felt.

Eleven

There were half a dozen cars parked in the courtyard, and the driver stopped in front of the garage. Despite his pounding heart Mason had the presence of mind to tip the guy, climbing out and pulling on his suit jacket, walking toward the front door, where a young woman in a cocktail dress greeted him.

"You can go through to the garden," she told him, smiling politely.

The foyer was empty, and he walked out to the garden, which was lit by festive strings of lights in the oak trees. The band space was set up at one side, not really a stage but on a low platform, raised just a few inches above the ground. None of the musicians were present, and the space wasn't lit yet, but the xylophone was set up, and the upright bass was waiting in its stand.

Just a few people were here so far, clustered at the bar, which was staffed by a woman in the same uniform as Ned. He should have planned to arrive later, he realized. In a smaller crowd he stood out more. It would have been wise to check in with Henry earlier too. Was he being sloppy here? His heart started to pound at the thought. No, he told himself, it was all going to work out.

He strolled over to the bar and asked for a tonic water. A woman in a colorful print dress, standing near the bar, greeted him, and he mumbled "Hello," shooting her a smile, but grabbed his drink and moved away to avoid conversation.

A few yards away he found a good vantage point, under a tree, where he stood and surveyed the group. There were no familiar faces, not yet. The men were all dressed business-casual rather than in evening wear. Hopefully he didn't look too out of place in a suit. Sam was really going to stand out when he got here.

Ned and another waiter came out of the kitchen, each carrying a rack of champagne flutes, and started setting them out on a table next to the bar. Ned spotted Mason and winked at him, all the while chatting quietly with his colleague. He worked quickly and deftly, flipping the flutes out of the rack and arranging them in neat rows. It was an admirable quality of Ned's, that he gave his best effort no matter what he was doing. Watching him work, he knew how lucky he was to be with the guy.

Hearing someone futzing with a drum kit, he looked to the band platform and saw the drummer, wearing a green jacket and clearly struggling to keep his warm-up routine unobtrusive. The guitarist wandered onto the stage, wearing the same retro green jacket and necktie, and then a woman appeared, in a sparkly pink gown and white elbow-length gloves, her hair in a anachronistic bouffant with a little white bow in it. It was Peggy, he realized, a grin spreading across his face. She had a tiny baby bump under the gown. It was barely detectable, but still part of the character, still kindred to Peggy Pregnant.

A few new faces had wandered in, and he scanned the crowd, sipping his tonic water. There was no sign of Margaret—or more important, Etor—but Henry had appeared, chatting with some people near the bar. He was wearing a brown linen suit with a green vest. Mason was grateful for that—he hadn't outdressed the host.

The woman he'd said hello to at the bar earlier appeared beside Mason.

"Cheers," she said, clinking her champagne flute against his glass. "Are you a Whitby?"

"No," Mason said, thinking quickly. "I work for Henry."

"So does my husband," she said, gesturing vaguely with the heel of her glass toward the bar. "You know, I love the way you've done your eyes.

What cosmetics line do you use?"

"Oh, I don't wear makeup," Mason said.

Her eyes narrowed, and she studied him for a moment. "OK," she said finally. "I think I need a refill."

She wandered back toward the bar, and Mason watched Henry, catching his eye as he stepped away from a conversation, nodding to him. As he approached, he had a puzzled little smile on his face.

"You look sharp," Mason said, glancing down at his vest.

"Mason?" Henry asked, surprised.

"Tonight, the name is Sam."

Henry grinned, and clinked his glass against Mason's. "You look so different. I was trying to fig-ure out who you were. Who did this to you?"

"A drag queen," Mason said casually. "I'm glad you didn't recognize me."

"I apologize for not getting back to you after your excursion to New Mexico. I've been busy. What did you find out?"

"In a nutshell, things aren't adding up. Manuel didn't write those letters to Margaret, at least not recently."

"That's it, then," Henry said, his eyes growing wide. "Etor is a fake."

"I have that feeling too, but let me try to get some tangible proof before we confront him on it. Where is he, anyway?"

His face clouded. "Rosalía says he's been with Mother all afternoon."

"Is there a chance they won't come down?"

"Mother tends to be reclusive, but she wouldn't miss this. She loves the attention. She'll make her entrance once there's a large enough crowd. I'm sure she'll bring Etor with her." Henry paused, looking around. "Where's your cousin?"

"He'll be here."

"I should go schmooze." He put a hand on Mason's forearm. "Let me know if you need anything," he said, and went toward the bar, instantly getting waylaid by a couple of women who greeted him by name.

Henry looked comfortable among his people, Mason thought, watching him for a moment. Hopefully Bart would see that too.

Mason sipped at his tonic water and looked around. More people were trickling in, and the garden was filling up. He exchanged perfunctory hellos when people caught his eye, but it was easy to lay low—he got less attention as a brunette than he ever did as a redhead.

Ned appeared at his elbow with a tray of canapés. "Snack treats, sir?"

"You're actually working," Mason said, scanning the tray.

"Of course I am. These are all vegan except the ones with the dead sea lice on top."

"Most people just call them shrimp," Mason said, and helped himself to one of the others.

Ned watched as Mason stacked canapés on his palm. "Did you skip lunch?"

231

"I guess I forgot to eat," Mason said through a mouthful. "These are good."

"Take a few more, then. These people aren't going to eat. In this demographic they're hyperfocused on staying thin." Ned surveyed the crowd. "I haven't seen Etor yet."

"Or Sam," Mason muttered darkly.

"I met Henry. You're right—he's totally gay. He was being very chatty with the servers in the kitchen when we were setting up. Only the men, though."

"Where's Bart?"

"He's not here yet, but I'll point him at Henry when I see him."

"You're not embarrassed to be bussing tables with your colleague here?"

"Not at all," Ned said. "I told him I was working undercover. And don't worry, he doesn't know any specifics."

"You should tell Bart not to talk to me—meaning don't talk to Sam."

"Did you see Peggy?" Ned asked.

"I love that outfit. She's less pregnant than usual, but she's still pregnant."

"It's hilarious, isn't it? She's playing the debutante." Ned scanned the crowd again. "I should go. The others will think I'm slacking."

After he'd gone, Mason finished the rest of his snacks, surveying the crowd. The garden was more crowded now, and the volume of conversation had risen. All four of Peggy's band members were onstage, wearing matching green jackets, and he could hear strains of their unamplified instruments warming up, the drums louder than the rest. He wandered over in front of their platform.

Peggy was talking to the drummer. "Do you see the little *p* on the sheet music?" she asked him. "It's right below where all the notes are."

"Oh, yeah," he said, examining the pages on his music stand.

"It means that we're playing calmly for people with pacemakers and nervous dispositions," she said. "Dial it back about fifty decibels."

"I'll get right on it," the drummer said, laughing.

Peggy glanced at Mason and said dismissively, "We'll be on in a few minutes, sir."

"Where are the computers?" he asked. "I don't see how you expect to make music without them."

"Mason?" she said, peering at him.

"Tonight I'm Sam, actually."

"I didn't recognize you. Damn, Billy is good." She stared at him for a few seconds, white-gloved hands on her hips. "Your hair looks like the Beatles, right before they grew it out. And if their hairdresser had been on tranquilizers."

He stifled a laugh. "It's not really my hair."

"I figured," she said, exasperated. More softly, looking past his shoulder, she added, "I haven't seen Etor."

"He'll come down when the matriarch does."

She nodded. "I'll keep my eyes peeled."

A man wearing a polo shirt and chinos

wandered up, leering at Peggy. "Such a pretty picture, the pink dress and the green jackets," he said, gesturing to encircle them with his arm. "You look like a chunk of ham in a bowl of spinach soup."

"Why, thank you," she said. "That's so appetizing. Yum, I'm getting hungry now." She leaned closer, and spoke to him in a confidential tone. "If you'll excuse us, sir, we're about to perform."

"Of course," he said, and stepped back.

Mason headed back to the bar for a refill. There had to be far more than Henry's predicted sixty people here now, he thought, standing in the bar line and surveying the space.

The band started up, and as Peggy had said it would be, the volume was set low. A few of the guests watched the band, but most continued with their conversations. The song was mellow, made even milder by the xylophone, and familiar, although it wasn't one of her songs. He recognized it when she started singing.

> Stormy weather
> Since my girl and I ain't together
> Keeps rainin' all the time.

She sounded great, and soulful, and he enjoyed the performance, stepping aside to watch. A few people clapped, Mason included, but most of the guests weren't paying attention.

"Thank you," Peggy said, and started into another number.

From the direction of the house he heard a

loud guffaw—he knew that laugh. Looking toward the foyer, he saw Sam, half a head taller than everyone else, a striking figure in the blue tux. Working his way through the crowd, he greeted people who had to be complete strangers, air-kissing a cheek here, giving a bro hug there, asking intently "How *are* you?" As Mason watched, he made his way to Henry, who reacted with familiarity, putting a hand on his shoulder. But then Henry did a double-take, looking confused, remembering it wasn't Mason.

Unable to overhear them, Mason watched intently as Sam spoke to him, standing much too close for Mason's liking. Henry was soon laughing, and slipped his arm around Sam's waist.

"Damn it," Mason said, and considered going over to interrupt them, but then thought better of it.

A smattering of applause went up for Peggy and the band, who had finished another song.

"Thank you," Peggy said, speaking into her mike and taking a little bow. She continued, her banter as smooth and agreeable as the sound of the xylophone. "In 1938, on the eve of the war, which I'm sure some of you here remember—thank you for your service," she said, and paused to clap delicately with her gloved hands, joined by a few others in the crowd.

It was humorous, Mason thought, glancing around the garden, because no one here was old enough to have participated in World War II, not even Margaret. There wasn't even anyone in a military uniform.

"In 1938," Peggy continued, "Cyrus Whitby had just completed this estate and was on his way to becoming a legitimate businessman. Prohibition and his lucrative gambling boat were fading into history. Props for Cyrus," she said, and paused to clap again, but it was a visual only, one hand grasping the mike, her white gloves making no sound. But more people had tuned in, evidenced by louder applause. "That very same year, on the other side of the world, William Butler Yeats found himself admiring a hot young tomato in a pub." With a flourish from the xylophone, she launched into a song.

> How can I, that girl standing there
> My attention fix
> On Roman or on Russian
> Or on Spanish politics?

Suddenly Sam was standing beside him, champagne flute in hand. "She's hilarious."

"What's a hot tomato?" Mason asked, tilting his head toward him.

"I assume it's 1938-speak for an attractive woman."

"I don't get what she's doing. She has a boyfriend, but she's singing about girls."

"Think of the whole image," Sam said, holding up his hands and framing her onstage, screwing one eye shut. "The pregnant debutante is a lesbian."

"So it's intentional?"

"It's her shtick. It's what she's always done—creating a persona. This one is making fun of rich people. The hilarious part is that they're standing here watching her, and they don't even know that."

"Did she tell you that's what she was doing?"

"No, man—look for yourself."

Mason looked at him. "You have an analytical mind."

"Thanks, bruh."

"Stop calling me that."

Sam laughed. "It's so easy to push your buttons."

"That's because you know where they're installed."

"So where's Etor?"

"Upstairs with Margaret. He'll be down when she comes down."

"Got it," Sam said. "I'll circulate and be prominent."

"Great, but stop flirting with Henry. We have someone picked out for him."

"That Bart guy? I guess they'd be cute together."

"Then lay off Henry. Maybe you could even steer them toward each other when Bart gets here."

"Fine," Sam said flatly. And before he walked away, added, "Uncle Buzzkill."

Peggy finished her song to polite applause, and Mason saw Deborah, wearing a pretty party dress with a poufy skirt, approach the stage.

"Oh, my god, that was so amazing," she gushed.

Peggy leaned down to talk to her, not using the mike. "Thank you, sweetheart."

Even though Peggy wasn't old enough to be matronly, especially in that getup, Deborah was unfazed.

"I love your makeup," she said. "You have to teach me how to do that."

"I'd love to," Peggy said. "What's your name?"

"Deborah."

"We're Peggy and the Plutocrats." She straightened up and spoke into the mike again. "This next song is dedicated to the lovely Deborah," she said, and signaled for the band to start.

> Fly me to the moon
> And let me play among the stars
> Let me see what spring is like
> On Jupiter and Mars.

True to his word, Sam was being visible, acting like he knew everyone, stepping into small group conversations, guffawing too loudly. It was unnerving to watch. Ned walked past with a tray of canapés and shot Mason a smile. He seemed to be working more than spying, but it didn't matter. Etor was nowhere to be seen.

The band segued into a xylophone solo, and when the song ended, Henry stepped over to the stage and spoke quietly to Peggy, who nodded. Was the band too loud, or had he figured out her satire?

But it wasn't that. Peggy spoke into the mike, much louder now, as someone had turned up the volume. She quickly commanded the attention of the assembled crowd.

"If I could have your attention, please … I'd like to introduce a woman who needs no introduction. Ladies and gentlemen … Margaret Whitby."

Margaret stepped into the garden to polite clapping, smiling broadly. She was transformed, her hair swept up in a stately pomp, a plush red off-the-shoulder gown, jewelry sparkling at her neck and her ears. On her arm, as if he had always been there, was Etor, in a black dinner jacket, smiling broadly, his hair even shinier than usual. The party guests surrounded her, greeting her excitedly, and she moved through them, murmuring acknowledgment, delicately clasping hands, renewing old acquaintances. This was definitely the matriarch, but how much Zoloft had it taken to get her down here?

Over by the bar, Sam caught his eye, and nodded toward the house. He was right—Mason wasn't here to gawk at Margaret. Taking a deep breath, he set his drink down and walked around the perimeter of the crowd, heading for the doorway into the foyer.

Bart was here, he saw, and he was standing close to Henry, one arm propped on the bar, and whatever he was saying had Henry grinning like an idiot. Seeing that made Mason's heart pound, even though this is what he'd wanted for them—intellectually, anyway. But he had other concerns right now.

The foyer was quiet when he went in, just a handful of people walking through toward the garden, and a bald guy in a dark suit, his hands folded in front of him. Despite the casual grin on his face, his eyes were sharp, assessing him as he approached. This was no blue blood, no office employee. He had to be security.

"Men's room?" the suit asked.

"I'm doing some work for Henry. The name's Mason."

"Oh, yes," he said, recognition sparking in his eyes. "Can I help with anything?"

"Actually, yeah—I'm going to be in this office for a few minutes," he said, gesturing to the door. "Don't let anyone wander in on me."

"You got it," he said, standing up a little straighter.

Mason opened the door to Henry's office, closing it quietly behind him. The room was dark, unoccupied, and the windows weren't visible from the garden, so he flipped on the light before he went to Henry's desk.

It felt unsavory to be doing this, and there was the risk that the suit would blab that Mason had been in here, but he needed to be sure about Henry. Sitting in the desk chair, he pulled open the bottom drawer. It was unlocked—either Henry was very trusting, or he had nothing to hide. He flicked through the files until he found the one with his name on it. Besides the nondisclosure form he'd signed, he was surprised to find a criminal record check and a credit report. Neither one was especially embarrassing, but thumbing through the paperwork, he could feel his face heating up. It felt like an invasion of privacy.

There was a file on Anna as well, thicker than the one for Mason. Besides her credit and criminal checks were a series of documents about her immigration process. No way was this stuff public record—Henry had dug into her background some other way. Several of the documents were dated two years back, probably when Anna had first started doing psychic readings for Margaret. She was originally Belarusian, he saw, flipping through the pages, but then decided he couldn't read any more—it was much too personal—and slid the file back in the drawer.

There was a thick file on Rosalía too, with more immigration paperwork. She was a citizen, naturalized a decade ago. The file on Eddie had the same lengthy criminal record that Mason had found, but the date of the query was over a year ago, probably when Henry had hired him. It seemed open-minded of him, at least, to hire a guy with that kind of baggage.

The other files in his desk were for people that he hadn't met, probably the groundskeepers and cleaners. They didn't seem to contain anything relevant, and more important, there was no evidence that Henry was colluding with Etor.

When he stepped into the foyer he caught the eye of a woman walking through, but she just smiled and continued on her way. Mason nodded to the security guard and then climbed the stairs, checking his phone once he reached the top, but there were no warning texts. As he was sliding his phone into his pocket he heard a muffled scream down the hallway. It was a woman's voice—Deborah? He'd seen her downstairs not long ago, but the sound had come from the direction of her room.

He strode quietly toward her door, which stood open a crack, and pushed it open a few inches. It was indeed Deborah, half naked and straddling a pale figure on the sofa, with a shock of blond hair—Eddy. Mason watched for a second to make sure he was seeing it accurately, but yes, that had been a cry of passion. They didn't notice him, and he pulled the door closed. It made no noise, not a squeak or a rasp. That was something to be thankful for—quality carpentry.

He wished he hadn't seen that. Why had they left the damn door open? Maybe she wanted to get caught. Eddy was exactly the right guy to pick if you wanted to upset your father. It explained Eddy's demeanor, he realized—he wasn't being suspicious and defensive because he was colluding with Etor, but rather because he was hiding his relationship with Deborah. That was a relief—Mason could forget about him.

After a quick check for text messages, finding none, he took a deep breath and opened the door to Etor's suite. He didn't turn on the light but used the dim glow of his phone screen to scan the room, looking for Etor's laptop. Logically he wouldn't hesitate to keep sensitive stuff on the computer, as it was secured, unlike his suitcases. He'd rather not paw through the guy's clothes, but he would if he couldn't find anything on the machine. He located the laptop in the bedroom, folded shut on the bed-side table.

Mason sat cross-legged on the floor, thinking that would keep the light away from the windows, and pulled it open. The lock screen appeared. His heart pounding, he tried the first set of numbers he'd gleaned from watching Etor, 9021.

"Password incorrect," it told him. "Try again."

He should have come up with another way to get into this thing, he realized. He hadn't even considered the possibility of failure. But there was still one other number. Fingers trembling, he typed 8921. It worked—he was looking at the desktop, a glossy image of sunset over a tree-lined lake. He heaved a sigh of relief and started clicking through Etor's documents.

There was a folder titled "Margaret," and another called "Manuel." He opened the Manuel file first, and immediately felt his heartbeat accelerate. A text file contained extensive notes about Manuel—all the information Mason had dug up over the last few days, including the name of the nursing facility in Alamogordo and his Alzheimer's diagnosis. The folder on Margaret had a file with notes about her family, and strangely, notes about Anna, including a rundown of a psychic reading done at her shop.

makes a stylized production of gazing into her
    crystal ball

> psychic reading was general impressions of the
>> dead, not direct spirit contact
> prodded her about her connection to high-value
>> clients; unwilling to talk about Margaret

That couldn't have been written by Etor—if he'd visited her shop, Anna would have remembered him when she met him here. He checked the metadata on the file. It had been created months ago, and the field for the author of the document said only "Amber S."

Closing it, he moved on to another folder, "Letters." It had high-resolution scans of pages written in Margaret's familiar hand. These were her letters to Manuel, he realized, from two decades ago, the responses to the letters she kept in her desk. How had Etor obtained these? The metadata on the file showed that they had been scanned over a year ago, and they were most definitely addressed to Manuel, not to Etor. That alone was proof positive that he was lying about arriving here from another world last week, and combined with the research he'd done on Margaret, Manuel, and Anna—the whole story was a lie.

Mason couldn't help but smile, and closed his eyes for a second, savoring the success. It was satisfying, almost a physical sensation—the lies crumbling and falling away, the truth settling in their place, shining and self-consistent and beautiful.

Looking to the screen again, he emailed the research files and the letters to himself, waiting impatiently for the few seconds they took to upload, then deleted the outgoing emails and closed the computer, returning it to its place on the bedside table. There was no point snooping through anything else—he had found enough.

Should he talk to Henry about it now, or wait until he was less preoccupied with his guests? Now, he decided. Given Etor's proximity to Margaret, it should be now.

Closing Etor's door behind him, he made his way to the back stairs, trotting down to the kitchen. The long island was strewn with foil trays, but the catering staff must have departed already, leaving only the waiters circulating outside. A lone figure stood at the island counter in a formal black-and-white maid's uniform, and turned toward him as he entered. He was startled to realize it was Rosalía; he'd never seen her dressed that way.

"Can I help you?" she asked, meeting his eye but not recognizing him.

Mason cleared his throat and tried to deepen his voice. "I'm looking for Henry."

"I think he took Margaret upstairs, He'll be back outside presently."

He grunted an acknowledgment, and Rosalía smiled politely, stepping out through the garden doors. Where was Etor, if Margaret had gone upstairs? Outside he could hear Peggy, not singing but talking over the sound of the party.

"Such a lovely evening," she was saying, "and so much champagne. Am I the only one who could go for a Greek coffee right about now?"

Greek coffee—with a start he remembered what that meant, but before he could move the garden door opened, and there was Etor. His eyes narrowed when he spotted Mason, and he paused to twist the deadbolt.

Mason's phone buzzed in his pocket, another warning—too late. Etor stepped closer, standing across the island from him.

"Why did you lock the door?" Mason asked, speaking in his deepened voice. "The waiters are going to need to get back inside."

"Who the fuck are you?" Etor demanded. All trace of his lilting European accent was gone.

"My name is, uh, Sam," Mason stuttered. "You seem to have forgotten your manners. Who are you?"

"You know exactly who I am. You've been on my computer."

"I have no idea what you're talking about." He could feel his cheeks burning, and wondered fleetingly whether it showed through the makeup.

Etor waggled his cell phone. "My login security took your picture when you bungled the password, you numbskull. How did you manage to figure it out?"

"Your computer photographed me?" Mason said, lapsing into his regular voice. "Technology is changing so quickly. It's hard to keep up."

"I know that voice," Etor said, peering at him now, his lip curling into a sneer. "I just saw you outside, in a blue tux. Your twin?"

"Something like that. In any case, I just had a good look at your research files, and I can tell you with confidence that the jig is up."

"That's pretty rash for a two-bit psychic. Let's think this through for a minute."

"What I don't get, Etor, or whatever your name is—you have money. All those bricks of cash are real. Why would you try to con Margaret?"

He scoffed. "That's chump change compared to her resources. It came from investors who believed I'd succeed and make them a huge return."

"Very clever," Mason said, hoping the flattery would keep him talking.

Etor smirked at him, flipping up the tails of his sleek black jacket and putting his hands on his hips. "You met one of them at the library."

"The guy in the fedora? How did he find me?"

"I slipped a GPS tracker into your backpack. You should clean that thing out once in a while. It's probably still in there."

"Seriously?" Mason said. "That's pretty creepy, but I must say, it shows impressive attention to detail."

Etor glanced to the doorway onto the garden, making sure they were alone. "You're not one of these people any more than I am. There'd be a huge cut for you if you keep your mouth shut and help me out. A fortune compared to the pittance that loser Henry is paying you."

Mason shook his head. "The project is doomed, man. If I figured it out, don't you think Henry would too?"

"Not if you reassured him otherwise," he said emphatically. "All you have to do is pronounce me legitimate. Tell them the spirits approve of Cousin Etor."

"Where did your passport come from? And Margaret's letters to Etor? They looked real."

"Forgeries," he said, shrugging. "Painstaking work by some talented people. I spent a lot of time prepping for this."

"So the letters from Manuel earlier this year were really from you."

Etor nodded, his eyes bright.

"Manuel hasn't lived in Spain for ages. How did you get the letters she sent to him there?"

"Do you have any idea how much postal workers get paid? They're predisposed to what you might call moonlighting."

"You paid one to intercept her mail," Mason said.

"See? You're not nearly as stupid as you look. Help me out, man—I'm so close, and the payoff is going to be huge."

"I know you're close. The whole package is very convincing. Margaret is completely on board."

Etor preened. "I got the idea when I robbed Manuel's house and found all those letters. The connection to a rich old woman was more valuable than anything else in the place."

"Is that where you're from? Alamogordo?"

"Don't question me," he snapped. "Why aren't

you more amenable to coming in on this? Psychic power is the biggest con job of them all."

"Not to me. I'll admit I almost bought the parallel universe thing."

"I watched the family for a while, and had my girlfriend talk to the chauffeur at an NA meeting. He spilled that the old gal talked to a psychic, and the idea came together from there."

"What's the next part of the plan? Get her to put you in her will?"

"That would work. Or she could just set up a trust fund. I'm not an unreasonable man."

"But you are a crook."

Etor's face hardened. "I get the feeling you're not going to help me."

Mason nodded. "That's correct."

Etor's face contorted with disgust. "It's only going to take me another week or two, and you're not going to stop me." Etor reached for the knife block on the island, drew out a paring knife, then cast it aside impatiently, pulling out a much bigger chef's knife, holding it up, a challenge in his eyes.

Etor was between him and the party, so Mason bolted for the other end of the kitchen, the island between them giving him a few seconds' head start. He went into the service hallway, and up the back stairs, taking them two at a time. Henry and Margaret were up here, Rosalía had said, and Etor wouldn't attack him in front of them.

He raced toward Margaret's door, elbows pumping, as fast as he could, not pausing to look back. As he reached for the handle of Margaret's door, the chef's knife clattered on the wall beside his head and fell to the floor. He burst into Margaret's room and slammed the door behind him, but there was no lock. Heart pounding, he searched the room, but there was no one here—he was trapped.

Etor pushed open the door and stood in the doorway, cautiously glancing around the room, uncertain what he'd find. Mason stood by the open window, panting. In the garden below, Peggy was singing again: "I love you / For sentimental reasons."

Etor stepped into the center of the room.

Mason took a couple steps toward him, and puffed out his chest. "Looks like you lost your weapon, little man."

Without taking a step, his lip curling into a sneer, Etor reached for a wine bottle on the table at the foot of Margaret's bed, among the remnants of her dinner. He swung the bottle over his head and struck it hard on the footboard, glass shards and cabernet flying.

"Ooh—is that red wine?" Mason asked him. "It'll stain the carpet."

Etor stepped toward him, holding the jagged bottle menacingly.

There was only one place to go. A narrow ledge ran outside the window, only a foot or so wide, but maybe he could climb back inside at the next room. He ducked through the open window and stepped out onto the ledge. The sudden proximity to the precipice made him freeze. He was high above the garden, Peggy and her band still performing, the party guests oblivious to him. Etor stuck his head out, so Mason forced himself to walk away from him, samurai-style, heel to toe, slowly, carefully. There were no other windows, just the sharp pitch of the roof on one side, the void of the garden far below on the other. He stopped and cautiously glanced back; Etor had stepped out behind him, the jagged bottle in his hand glinting in the light from the party.

Walking as quickly as he could, Mason reached the end of the roof, but there was nowhere else to go—the ledge ended abruptly, and he couldn't climb the steep shingles. Turning around, he faced Etor, who was approaching warily, his bravado waning in the face of the danger.

From far away he heard his own voice call out: "Roundhouse kick." He glanced down at the garden. Just one face was turned upward, over the blue sheen of his tux, looking at him: Sam. He nodded encouragement and gestured, twisting his forearm in a loop.

The roundhouse kick. That was an old memory. One summer, before he'd even hit puberty, his uncle had decided Mason needed to butch up, and had taken him to karate lessons. Not much of it had stuck, but he remembered that kick, how it felt, swinging his foot around, rotating his body, the ball of his preteen foot connecting with the sensei's thigh.

Etor was advancing, seconds from lashing out, throwing Mason off the roof into the garden below. He could see himself falling, flailing wildly, but he quickly pushed that image away and took a deep breath, concentrating on time—slowing it down, clearing his head, sharpening his focus. Sam was right. That kick was still available, still resided in his muscle memory.

Etor lunged at him, moving in slow motion now in Mason's altered state of mind, the jagged dark-green glass aimed at his face, his intention to send Mason backward into the abyss. As the ugly weapon came at him, Mason rotated on one foot, focused on Etor's elbow, and landed the kick, nimbly maintaining his own balance. Etor's face shifted from hard resolve to surprise—he hadn't expected that. The bottle flew out of his hand, tumbling in a graceful arc toward the garden below. It seemed to take minutes, with everything happening at this pace, but eventually Mason heard it smash on the paving stones below.

His eyes wide, Etor's body twisted with the kick, but his momentum carried him toward Mason, even more slowly than before. After landing the kick, Mason was positioned sideways, and even though he could only react in slow-motion, his mind was working faster, and he calmly bent his knees, squatting toward the shingles on the roof to dodge the trajectory of Etor's mass. Etor's shoulder grazed his belly, twisting the flap of his suit jacket, and Mason wobbled a little on his feet, but he had avoided the blow, and kept his balance.

Etor sailed off the ledge, disappearing into the darkness, followed ages later by a sickening thud, and after that, screaming and commotion among the party guests.

Mason felt dazed, but he pulled his mind back to normal speed and looked down at the garden. Etor's frame lay motionless on the paving stones, a twisted mass of black and white, like a broken penguin. People crowded around him, a couple of them squatting near his head. Etor's foot twitched. Maybe he wasn't dead.

There was a bit of sparkly pink in the crowd, pushing toward the body—Peggy, and her band-mates in green, the xylophonist still holding his mallets. Henry stood back by the bar, his torso twisted away, unable to look, his hands over his face. Bart was with him, a hand on his shoulder, his attention on Henry rather than the broken pen-guin, the focus of the rest of the crowd. Marga-ret was farther back, beyond the bar, crimson and sparkly, being kept away from the commotion by a small group of people. Only Sam was looking up at Mason, staring steadily, a wry grin on his face.

Inhaling deeply, he walked back along the ledge to Margaret's window. It seemed even more treach-erous now, and he took his time so as not to stum-ble. He couldn't believe he'd practically run along it a minute ago. How silly would it be to fall off now, when he wasn't being chased? The adrenaline rush ebbing, he concentrated on not tumbling off, and eventually made it inside.

The next hour was a blur. One of Henry's plain-clothes security guards, the bald guy in the suit that he'd spoken to earlier, met him upstairs and detained him, polite but firm. Weirdly, he escorted Mason into Etor's suite and parked him on the sofa. The guard's intention was to isolate him until the police arrived to interview him, to prevent his story getting contaminated with other witnesses' details, but Sam pushed his way in, claiming "Dude—he's my brother."

He brought Mason a bottle of water, which he guzzled.

"Nice roundhouse," Sam said.

"I'd forgotten about that."

"I didn't," Sam said. He seemed softer now, gentler than before. "You know, I think I'm done."

"For good?" Mason asked quietly, glancing briefly at the guard.

"I've accomplished what I set out to do—I helped save your neck. So, yeah."

"Will I see you again?"

"Of course. You know where I'll be. Maybe you'll need me again one day."

"Do you still have my credit card?"

Sam begrudgingly pulled it out of his pants pocket and handed it over. "Later, bruh," he said, and was gone.

Two cops appeared and spent a long time interviewing him, their questioning much more intense than Matt's interrogation had been, just a few days ago in the same room. Finally they seemed satisfied, and the one who'd asked most of the questions folded her notebook closed.

"I think that clears things up for now," she said. "Are you going to be all right?"

Mason was surprised at the sudden show of concern. "I'm OK," he said. "Have you spoken to Henry? He looked completely shaken up."

"He was pretty distraught," she said. "Apparently his wife did the same thing."

"What thing?"

"I talked to the housekeeper," the other cop said. "The wife did a swan dive off a parking structure at the hospital where she was diagnosed with cancer."

"My god," Mason said. "That's horrible."

"Good thing we have the death with dignity law now. Too late for her, though."

Mason followed them downstairs into the kitchen, where Ned and Peggy were waiting, both sitting on the island amid the forgotten foil food trays. Rosalía was perched on a stool near the sink, arms folded. Ned jumped down when they came in, and gave Mason a tight hug.

"Are you OK?" he asked, pulling back and studying Mason's eyes.

"I'm fine. Where did everybody go?"

"The party broke up when you threw that guy off the roof," Peggy said.

"I didn't throw him," Mason said intently. "He tried to throw me." To his relief the cop just grinned at Peggy's comment as she and her partner left. "Where's Henry?"

"He was traumatized," Ned said. "Bart's with him. I'm glad he came—he seemed to know what to do. Where's Sam? He said he was going to see you upstairs an hour ago."

"He left."

Ned just nodded, but Peggy shot him a questioning look.

"I don't think we're going to see him for a while," Mason said.

Twelve

The following Thursday, the weather finally warming up for summer, Mason locked up his bicycle outside Miss Cassie's office, and was soon seated in his usual place.

"It was so interesting to meet Sam," Cassie began, glancing up from her notes.

"You did a full session with him?" he asked.

"Two, actually."

"I hope he wasn't talking about me the whole time."

"He provided a lot of insight into you, and your childhood. Things you haven't come up with yourself."

"I wish he hadn't done that," Mason said,

scowling.

"Have you heard of a condition called dissociative identity disorder?"

He shook his head.

"It's when a person has two sets of personality traits that appear at different times, manifested as different people, who don't remember each other's actions."

"I don't have that," he said firmly. "I know he looks like me, but he's not me."

"He looks exactly like you. When he came in, he was wearing a green track suit and red mirror sunglasses. Do you have a green track suit, or did you happen to find one at home?"

"He's not me," Mason insisted. He had, in fact, found the track suit, along with the sunglasses, the tux, and a bunch of other clothes in a black trash bag blocking the front door, late on the night they'd come home from the Whitby Spring Affair. But that didn't prove what she was implying. "Ned saw Sam and I together. Lots of people did."

"All right," she said, scribbling notes and shifting in her seat. "If he's your cousin, who's his mother? When did you last see her?"

"Miss Cassie, I promise you I don't have disproportionate identity disorder."

"Dissociative," she corrected.

"Right."

"You said he won't bother me again. Where did he go?"

"I don't know," he said helplessly. "But I'm not crazy."

"No one said that," she said, holding up a palm.

"Not in those words, but that's the implication."

She studied him for a moment. "Even if Sam really were your 'cousin,'" she said, waggling her fingers to put the word in air quotes, "let's talk about his personality."

"Well, he's way more confident than I am. I admire that, in a way. But he also rubs me wrong way—he was way too flirty with Ned."

She nodded, resuming her notes, and they talked about Sam. Regardless of what she believed, it felt good to unload about how frustrating the guy was.

Riding the metro to NoHo, he thought about Miss Cassie's assessment of Sam. She was dead wrong that Mason had a dissociated personality, but maybe she was half right—maybe he was suppressing some part of himself that had manifested in Sam. Maybe Sam had appeared for reasons beyond helping out at the party. He thought about the trash bag full of clothes, left on the front step like a bag of leaves. That track suit, and the fake gold jewelry—he'd never wear stuff like that. But the tux looked sharp, and he might even be able to pull off the red jeans.

Rosalía greeted him warmly at the gate to Clementine Manor, buzzing him in. That was gratifying, he thought, the first warmth he'd felt from her. The town car was parked in front of the garage and Eddy, dressed in jeans and a T-shirt, was detailing it with a bucket and a rag. He watched Mason suspiciously as he parked his bicycle.

"How about this weather, huh?" Mason called to him as he walked toward the house, not waiting for a response.

Henry looked up when he stuck his head into his office, then stood, greeting Mason like an old friend and waving him over.

"Sit," Henry bellowed, ever the businessman.

"I should probably apologize for ruining your party," Mason said as he dropped into one of the chairs in front of the desk.

Henry laughed. "It was worth it to find out who Etor really was. The police said he has an extensive criminal record, stretching from Minnesota to Los Angeles."

"Will he be charged with anything?"

"Fraud, at least," Henry said. "Maybe more once he's out of the hospital. They don't incarcerate people before they're discharged, because they don't want to assume the costs of their medical treatment."

"What about his accomplices? He sent one to intimidate me at the library."

"Hopefully he'll identify them too."

"Well, I'm glad we figured it out."

"You figured it out," Henry said. "And you certainly brought fresh air to the Spring Affair.

Deborah was quite enamored of the Plutocrats."

"Which ones?"

"The band," Henry said. "Peggy and the Plutocrats."

"Of course," Mason said. He'd forgotten about that. "How's Margaret?"

"Upset. Heartbroken, in a way, I think. But eventually she'll be thankful."

"I don't suppose I can talk to her."

"Maybe another time. She's still recovering."

"It feels incomplete, not debriefing her," Mason said.

"Celebrate the success, Mason. Enjoy it." Henry held his gaze. "We're all so busy with the processes, the doing and becoming, we forget to just be."

"That sounds insightful. I'll try."

Henry pulled a check register out of his desk and flipped it open. "I'll pay you for seven days, from your consult through the party," he said. "Were there any other expenses?"

"Three hundred for Matt's work," he said, and rattled off what he'd paid Anna, and the cost of the mirror, and Billy's fee.

Henry nodded.

Watching him write, Mason said, "You were pretty shaken up that night."

"It was quite a shock," Henry said, not looking up. "I know it wasn't your fault. I was lucky that one of the party guests was able to calm me down."

"I'm glad."

"I've actually seen him twice since then. I think we might even be dating."

"That's great news, man."

Henry tore off the check and looked up. "You might have seen him here that night."

"Maybe," Mason said vaguely. "I was pretty busy."

Henry grinned. "Mason, it was my party. I know you invited Bart, and I know it was a setup. And I'm grateful."

Henry rose to slide the check across his vast desk, and Mason thanked him, stuffing it in his backpack.

Walking him to the front door, Henry said, "Thanks for saving Mother a lot of money and heartache."

Mason grinned. "It was fun," he said, and said good-bye.

Cycling down the hill, he thought about that. It had been fun—and terrifying too, but mostly fun. What a way to make a living.

Also from Dagmar Miura

The Mason Braithwaite Paranormal Mystery Series

In the previous books in the series, no one is ever quite sure whether psychic investigator Mason gets results with actual psychic power or his more mundane flatfooting, but the disheveled redhead manages to resolve some intractable mysteries.

mason.dagmarmiura.com

The Slater Ibáñez Books

Don't mess with the hothead—or he might just mess with you. Slater is only interested in two kinds of guys: the ones he wants to punch, and the ones he sleeps with. Things get interesting when they start to overlap.

slater.dagmarmiura.com

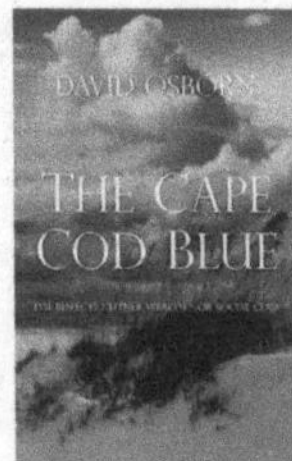

The Cape Cod Blue

The glittering, exalted world of art auctioning hides love, hate, and parricidal murder in a wealthy and socially prominent family when forgery of an anonymous Cape Cod painting is used to steal a world-famous portrait that's worth a fortune.

capecod.dagmarmiura.com

The Bone Bridge

Yarrott Benz, the 2016 Ippy Award winner for memoir, is forced to deal with extraordinary self-sacrifice in this harrowing account of teenage brothers, as different as night and day, trapped together in a dramatic medical dilemma.

bonebridge.dagmarmiura.com